RENEWALS 458-4574

DATE DUE

GAYLORD			PRINTED IN U.S.A.

There a Petal Silently Falls

Weatherhead Books on Asia

WEATHERHEAD EAST ASIAN INSTITUTE, COLUMBIA UNIVERSITY

Weatherhead Books on Asia

WEATHERHEAD EAST ASIA INSTITUTE, COLUMBIA UNIVERSITY

Literature DAVID DER-WEI WANG, EDITOR

Ye Zhaoyan, *Nanjing 1937: A Love Story*, translated by Michael Berry (2003)
Oda Makoto, *The Breaking Jewel*, translated by Donald Keene (2003)
Han Shaogong, *A Dictionary of Maqiao*, translated by Julia Lovell (2003)
Takahashi Takako, *Lonely Woman*, translated by Maryellen Toman Mori (2004)
Chen Ran, *A Private Life*, translated by John Howard-Gibbon (2004)
Eileen Chang, *Written on Water*, translated by Andrew F. Jones (2004)
Writing Women in Modern China: The Revolutionary Years, 1936–1976, edited by
    Amy D. Dooling (2005)
Han Bangqing, *The Sing-song Girls of Shanghai*, first translated by Eileen Chang,
    revised and edited by Eva Hung (2005)
Loud Sparrows: Contemporary Chinese Short-Shorts, translated and edited by Aili Mu,
    Julie Chiu, Howard Goldblatt (2006)
Hiratsuka Raichō, *In the Beginning, Woman Was the Sun*, translated by Teruko Craig
    (2006)
Zhu Wen, I Love Dollars *and Other Stories of China*, translated by Julia Lovell (2007)
Kim Sowol, *Azaleas: A Book of Poems,* translated by David McCann (2007)
Wang Anyi, *The Song of Everlasting Sorrow: A Novel of Shanghai*, translated by
    Michael Berry with Susan Chan Egan (2008)

History, Society, and Culture CAROL GLUCK, EDITOR

Takeuchi Yoshimi, *What Is Modernity? Writings of Takeuchi Yoshimi*, translated with
    an introduction by Richard Calichman (2005)
Contemporary Japanese Thought, translated by Richard Calichman (2005)
Overcoming Modernity, Yasuda et al., translated by Richard Calichman (2008)

COLUMBIA UNIVERSITY PRESS ▽ NEW YORK

THREE STORIES BY *Ch'oe Yun*

TRANSLATED BY **BRUCE** AND **JU-CHAN FULTON**

There a Petal Silently Falls

Columbia University Press wishes to express its appreciation of support by the
Korea Literature Translation Institute toward the publication of this book.

This publication has been supported by the Richard W. Weatherhead Publication
Fund of the Weatherhead East Asian Institute, Columbia University.

Columbia University Press
Publishers Since 1893
New York   Chichester, West Sussex

Library of Congress Cataloging-in-Publication Data
Ch'oe, Yun, 1953–
[Chŏgi sori ŏpshi han chŏm kkonnip i chigo. English]
There a petal silently falls : three stories / by Ch'oe Yun ; translated by Bruce and
Ju-Chan Fulton.
    p. cm. — (Weatherhead books on Asia)
ISBN 978-0-231-14296-0 (cloth : alk. paper) — ISBN 978-0-231-51242-8 (electronic)
I. Fulton, Bruce.   II. Fulton, Ju-Chan.   III. Ch'oe, Yun, 1953– Soksagim
soksagim. English.   IV. Ch'oe, Yun, 1953– Yŏlse kaji irŭm ŭi kkot hyanggi.
English.   V. Title.
PL992.18.Y86C4613   2008
895.7'34—dc22   2007037906

Columbia University Press books are printed on permanent and durable acid-free
paper.
This book was printed on paper with recycled content.
Printed in the United States of America
c 10 9 8 7 6 5 4 3 2 1

Contents

There a Petal Silently Falls   1

Whisper Yet   79

The Thirteen-Scent Flower   115

AFTERWORD   189

There a Petal Silently Falls

There a Petal Silently Falls

As you pass by the grave sites scattered throughout the city, you may encounter her, a girl whose maroon velvet dress barely covers her, a girl who lingers near the burial mounds. Please don't stop if she approaches you, and don't look back once she's passed you by. If your eye should be drawn to the flesh showing between the folds of that torn, soiled dress, or drawn to something resembling a wound, walk away with downcast eyes as if you hadn't seen a thing. But if you're a man in your twenties with the piercing gaze that sometimes accompanies that age, she will follow you, her long, stringy, dusty hair crowned with a withered garland; perhaps she will look at you with eyes that have lost their focus, smile at you with a smile more crimson than the flowers in her hair. And when in spite of herself she pulls at your jacket or elbow and draws close to you like a magnet, please be as gentle as possible when you remove her hand. You need not be afraid of her, you need not threaten her and rush off. All you have to do is look into her face for a moment and show some interest.

We know you're busy, but if you can spare a few minutes, you might just gently stroke her cheeks with their smudges of face powder and chaos of purple lipstick. Please don't raise your voice, and when she reaches for you with dirty fingers, try not to make fun of her or curse her. Don't be too quick to sympathize with this wasted girl who longs to escape the shadows for the sunlight, and if she retreats from your indifference or from a smile or gesture you may have let slip, don't spit on her footprints as if she were bad luck—even if she blocks your path for a moment, even if you feel a blind urge to escape your predicament by assaulting her, knocking her down, stomping on her, strangling her, disposing of her without a trace. Because even if you do all this, many other girls will notice a young man like you. Traumatized and deranged, they will follow you, crying "Brother!"

1

Fourteen? Fifteen? Yeah, fifteen at the outside.

This supposition, based on the meager outline of the chest beneath the girl's cotton T-shirt, left the man feeling somewhat less than comfortable. The girl looked like she was drunk and she followed close behind him, breathing heavily. She held a small cloth bundle to her side. Her expression was difficult to read. Was that a smile on her face?

A certain year, a certain month, a certain day. Exactly three in the afternoon.

No one else was at the riverside near the construction site. The bucket of a power shovel lingered menacingly in the air, threatening to drop.

In the still of the seething sun the girl had stood on the flight of steps leading from the road down to the river. Her face had an alcohol flush, and perhaps she longed for the shade that sliced across the midpoint of the stairway. Her gaze had detected the man and his shadow moving silently far off to the right. She had hopped over the KEEP OUT sign that was posted halfway, and hastened down the remaining steps. When she was almost at the bottom the man had passed by, unaware that someone was there, someone who had bounded down the slope as quietly as an animal.

Spurred by the pulse drumming in her temples, the girl had caught up to the man and begun following close behind his imposing back. If it had been someone else instead, she might have followed him as well. She labored to keep up, and the panting she was trying to control finally exploded in one great gasp. For the first time the man turned back, and there he saw the source of this violent outpouring of breath: a face he would one day curse and strike, and later a face of suffering and longing, but now dry and pinched in spite of the indications of alcohol. The man came to a halt and so did she, and when he looked down into her face, a half-smoked cigarette sticking out from his large, protruding teeth, his gaze cold enough to chill the hot sunlight, she looked up at him.

Impassive, the man resumed walking. The girl followed, three feet behind, trying desperately to control her stumbling feet. It was as if the man had ordered her to keep a strict distance between them. The man could hear her pant, but he didn't stop or look back. He didn't demand to know why a girl of her age, drunk in broad daylight, was hanging around a construction site where only workers were allowed; he didn't ask why she followed him so doggedly. He'd seen plenty of girls stumbling around drunk like this one. They might have had a reason, but why should he care? There was no need to shoo her away; in his mind these girls might as well have been nonexistent.

Instead of following the river before climbing to the road, the man, as he usually did, entered a sloping grove bordered by dense scrub: a dry tangle of trees covered with dust from the traffic passing above, the green foliage unusually dark for this time of year, a growth dense enough to swallow up all traces of a car or truck that might have strayed from the roadway. Later the man would say that unlike on other days, he hesitated at those woods. But he had nothing specific in mind before he entered them; it was just that something about them seemed odd that day, so odd he forgot for an instant the girl who meekly followed him like an animal would its trainer. The slope seemed especially steep, and in his weary state he squatted midway up and lit another cigarette.

He looked again at the girl and wondered for the briefest instant why she was following him around like some mad dog. And then he noticed her shabby appearance as she gazed toward the river, now practically hidden by the undergrowth around them. Sensing his gaze, she turned halfway toward him and produced a chilling smile, and a few words tumbled, indecipherable, from her lips.

There was something about her for which the man lacked words, something that prevented him even from seeing her as pretty or ugly. The world inhabited by her small body was utterly different from the world the man knew, and instinctively his muscles tightened in response. The noise from the traffic on the pavement above pounded in his temples, provoking him, translating his discomfort into visceral fear. Perhaps he was a creature of habit, a man for whom all feelings were reduced to physical reactions, who used aggression to dissipate any sort of visceral fear.

In one violent spasm of motion, as if trying to escape from a trap, he fell upon the girl from behind, the girl whose smile, if he could call it that, came from a world he didn't understand. He had an illusion that the girl was mocking him; he thought he heard an annoying giggle. As if to strip that laughter of its thick shell, but at the same time perplexed at the ease with which he removed her tattered clothing, he attacked her meager body. It was an act of escape and confirmation. The man lingered only briefly in the depths of a dark cavity that offered neither dissolution nor pleasure. The instant he imagined the girl's laughter ceasing, he pushed her away with a shudder. She lay prone, no laughter, no movement, gasping, still clutching her small round cloth bundle.

Silence fell over them. Perhaps the man was apprehensive about what he had just done. Or perhaps, looking around and finding no one in sight, he momentarily entertained the notion of doing away with this girl who lay there so drunk and relaxed. But something dissuaded him, something he didn't understand. *Look at her face. Nothing scary about it. You'd almost think she's happy. Look, she's humming. But there's something strange about those eyes, something wild—must be the booze.* Before he knew it the monotone of her humming had stopped. Her eyes were closed. Was it possible? Was she asleep? Quietly as he could the man rose. *Get out of here. She'll never remember your face.* But he had miscalculated. Before he could take a step the girl had lurched to her feet, ready to follow him. Her lips wore an incipient smile that seemed to say she had read his mind. Again he tensed.

Before long the girl was following the man at the same three-foot distance as before. When they arrived at the basement room where he lived, not far from where they had encountered each other, the girl slipped inside, shielding her head as if from a barrage of stones. The liquor flush left her face, and by the time her eyes adjusted to the darkness of the cramped, shedlike room she was drowsy and her eyes were half shut. She curled up in the corner on the bare floor and lay there in a sacklike heap, limbs motionless, until the following morning when the man kicked her in the side once, twice, three times. During the night, afraid she would die in her sleep, he had thought of waking her and sending her off before such a horrible event should come to pass. The girl was snoring gently, though, and he had gone back to sleep, wondering helplessly how his life could suddenly have gotten so fouled up.

Later he would say that the girl was bad luck from the start. She moved silently like a mouse, and when he threw her around, made her yield to him, when he cursed or struck her, she soaked it all up like a sponge, shrinking and expanding in time with the commands that issued from his fitful mood swings. Her existence triggered in him a feeling of powerlessness without cause, anger without object. The months he spent with her were hell, he would say, and even after she had disappeared from his sight that hell continued in another form.

The thing he couldn't stand was her silence. More than a month had passed since she had followed him home, and not once had she opened her mouth or set foot outside. At first he thought she had escaped from somewhere—a reformatory, perhaps—or was running away from something she had done. Such things were possible. But he didn't bother to question her. She wouldn't have answered, and if he had pressed her she would have feigned ignorance. She had made a nest, you might say, in that spot to which she had crawled that day, the corner of the renovated storage room where the man lived, and she stayed in no other place, at least as long as the man remained there. Every time the man left, he locked her in. And for some reason he himself couldn't understand, he added a second lock to the bottom of the door. Perhaps he was afraid she might dart outside and do something that would put him in a fix. Or maybe he was sensitive to what his neighbors might see, or felt pressured to isolate the girl, as if she carried a virulent disease. But for the man these reasons weren't important; what was important was that the girl had shown no reaction the past several weeks to these intuitive measures, had merely remained in her nest, legs drawn up beneath her, observing his every movement as if she was keeping watch over him when he slept and ate. In so doing she turned their brief encounters sour.

Again the man was tempted to thrash the girl, who now made her presence known by a foul odor. He was tempted to strip that bony, unattractive body like he would pluck a bird, and then put her out. He felt intensely, soaringly violent whenever he saw her, and ultimately he lacked the superhuman effort necessary to control these impulses. It scared him the way he could beat her down and she would sit back up like a trampled blade of grass, no change in her expression, so instead of striking her, he would roar and shout until he had exhausted himself. For a time he went out of his way not to provoke her. She was dirty, frightening, awful.

The man returned home drunk to find her curled up on a piece of plastic in the corner. She didn't so much as flinch at the sound of his arrival. The sight of her filled him with dread, made his hair stand up, and he felt as if the intoxication that had spread throughout his limbs was suddenly being swept away. Immediately he filled a washbasin and dashed the water over her wretched body. When he had done this several times she shuddered and sat up, eyes shut. As if peeling off her skin, she stripped away the shreds she wore—it was no longer possible to call them clothes—and his drunken gaze was jarred by the sight of her emaciated arms and the bruises that covered the insides of her thighs.

All at once the girl's eyes snapped open. As if possessed, she herself began pouring water over her bony form, a fuzzy outline taking shape in a developing photo, until her teeth chattered and her skin had turned blue to the pores, until she had emptied the basin. And then her hand darted to the floor and found a piece of broken cement, and with a bestial, unrestrained burst of energy she began to scratch at her flesh in a quick, convulsive rhythm. The jagged fragment crisscrossed her inner thighs, her belly, the small of her back, her calves, etching crimson lines. By the time the first traces of blood had appeared, her hands had slashed and danced all over her hopelessly meager body. She was a canvas splattered with crimson, a red mosaic with a ghastly mottling of white where her hands hadn't touched. Finally, with a strangled shriek, she slumped to her side like a blood-soaked bundle of firewood.

Terrified, the man could not confront the nightmare taking place before his eyes. Anxiously, like a criminal removing evidence, he hoisted the girl's lukewarm body and dumped her in his part of the room. There he stuffed the neck of a bottle of liquor into her mouth with enough force to have broken her teeth, as if to stifle her faintest breath. Imprisoned with the girl in this fathomless night, he held the bottle in place with mortal intensity until every last drop of liquid had flowed down her tensed throat. And then he waited. How long did that frightening vigil last: five minutes? Five hours? An eternity? Gradually a fragmentary illusion became an accomplished fact that possessed his simple mind. In the extremity of his fear, the girl's hands dancing madly over her bony form were transformed into his hands, and the violent, convulsive rhythm of her assault upon herself was transferred to the rhythm of aggression boiling inside him. The sight of her stretched out like a log frightened him. Why in this situa-

tion had he resorted to assaulting the girl? At what moment
had that first wave of violence surged over him? Glaring
coldly at his knotted hands, he tried to remember, and once
again there appeared in his mind the vivid scene of his fists
punishing her body, beating an insane tattoo to the command
of something shameful and evil that lurked inside him.

Finally a crimson flush rose from the girl's neck to her face.
Her lips opened wide, exposing her yellowish teeth. Her harsh
breathing produced a poisonous stink. Her pupils were vacant. Perhaps the man and the girl were intuitively aware at
that moment that each of them had passed a critical point.

They would pass that point several times, but going in different directions. Perhaps each instant was a critical point. Or
perhaps it was as if the soil beneath each step of their wavering shadows was mined and they couldn't distinguish one
step from the next. Again the man looked avidly at the hideous crimson wounds, at the sticky, fragile clots. Afterward
he would find that those wounds were everywhere visible—in
the infinite sky, in the riverside sandbanks, in a bowl of rice,
and later in the girl's healed flesh. That night he made love
with those shameful wounds, which would last forever as
scars. Through the slits of her eyes the girl gazed at the darkened paper covering the ceiling. Again her mouth opened
wide, and out came a peculiar sound that might have been a
laugh. Or perhaps a moan.

2

How many nights has it been? Dozens? Hundreds? . . . Here
it is dark again. It wants to be dark, everywhere dark. . . . And
all I want is sleep. What is it with me? I have to wake up. This
instant. I pinch myself—no feeling. I pinch and twist—not a

drop of blood. I've walked, oh how I've walked, you'd think I'd have broken a toe, but no. My innards, they're cursed. I have to begin. I really must. But begin what?

It's summer already. Or maybe the end of summer? Back then it must have been late in the spring. I'm farther and farther away. But from what? And I'm going too fast. Why is the sky so hazy? It's smoke, that's what it is, covering everything. Doesn't matter how far I walk, that hazy sky is always there, following me. Look—coming out of the sun, that black dust, coal dust. My head's spinning. I'm dizzy. Maybe I should eat. But I'm sick to my stomach and the sick feeling won't go away. And there's that stink I've never noticed before. . . . It's coming from *me*, I'm sure of it. Even when it rains. I thought the rain would wash it away, but no. Where did that stink come from? It's in me now, it's in my blood, and they're not going to leave me alone. Maybe they'll all go crazy because of me.

It's hard to breathe. Someday they'll lock me up, they'll crush my face and throat, they'll cover me with a thick coat of paint. Disappear . . . that's what I should have done. Then I wouldn't hear the whispers anymore. And the photos that keep dancing in front of me, clicking like a movie projector.

How long has it been since that day? A month? Two months? If my legs were longer, my arms stronger. . . . It's awful, this heart of mine, still beating as if it didn't care, still cracking!

Mama, folded in half, all those holes in her. . . . How does a person get holes in her so fast? . . . And then it was over.

What was that I said just now? "Mama." My mama. Mama with holes in her. If I had run faster, if I had been quicker to get free of that arm that caught me . . . would everything be different now? "Stay put no matter what," Mama said when she nudged me into that gloomy alley that leads to the market. "I'll come back for you tonight."

I ran out of the alley; I didn't want to lose sight of her. What were we doing there? Mama, like a scarecrow spinning around, no scream, just a hacking sound, and then she dropped. Mama, sprawled out, jostled by people milling around, blood shooting out of her, no time to focus her gaping eyes before I ran to her. What were we doing there, Mama and I? All I know is that wherever the neighbors gathered, murmuring and whispering, Mama was there, head lowered, attentive.

I couldn't see how many holes there were, or how they were made. By the time she took my hand and I felt the joints of her fingers, the blood was pouring out of her. How strongly she held my hand! But those holes—the moment I realized there were holes in Mama, a black curtain drifted over me. I wonder if I just fell to the ground, Mama still clutching my hand? . . . I've asked myself that question thousands of times. After that curtain, nothing. People swarming. People crying out. Cries that came from the depths of the earth.

What did I do that morning? And the day before? And the day before that? All my memories dried up and disintegrated behind the black curtain that fell over my eyes. What day was it? All those people. That jumble of faces. What were Mama and I doing there? What made us go to that spot? Mama and I were wearing our Sunday best—we only had one such outfit—like we were going out for a big dinner at someone's house, or maybe a picnic. . . . We took a bus, didn't we? To get downtown you have to take a bus. I can't remember which one we took, who was on it, whether we talked. Who did we see on the way to the bus stop? While we waited at the bridge for the bus that would take us across the river and downtown, did Mama visit the hole-in-the-wall shop like she usually did and ask Mr. Pak about his wife? Mr. Pak's wife was sick in bed. Or maybe no one was on the street—just like no one's on the street that's appeared in my mind. Maybe Mr. Pak closed down his shop and went home to tend to his wife. I've never been so far away before. I can't go back there. Even if I wanted to.... No, it's impossible. With Mama gone now, who would talk to me? A lot of the neighbors must have seen me running after Mama and crying; if they see me now, coming back by myself, they'll point at me and say things. I'm all alone now. I have been ever since that day.

What happened? How come Mama and I were all dressed up like we were going to a big party? ... Can't I get rid of that black curtain hanging there in my mind? Everything and everyone is all jumbled up; all I can do is ask questions. But there aren't any answers. My hand that Mama grabbed so desperately. Her hand closing on mine, crushing it. I think her lips were moving.... I think she was going to say something about Brother.

In the emptiness of my mind there's only a cold wind. Then, we were downtown in order to see Brother? No, I must be crazy. Didn't Mama tell me he was dead? She didn't mention a thing to me the night those strange men came to our house; all she did was hug me and wail, but something came out from her that told me Brother was dead. Last fall two men in suits sat down on the edge of our veranda and waited for Mama to come home from the market. They must have told her. Mother started shrieking at them; her voice was all choked up and no one could understand her; and the next thing I knew, the whole neighborhood was there. I was so embarrassed I hid in my room. I don't know what those men said, but I felt they were lying. Mama screamed at those men, then grabbed them. I watched from the door to my room. One man's sleeve ripped and the other man slipped after Mama grabbed his pants leg.

Mama squirmed all over; then she plopped down and rocked back and forth like Hyang-sun's dog, like she was struggling against something; then she started banging her head on the floor. I ran out to stop her, but when she saw the men in suits trying to leave, she jumped up and threatened them with a stick. Since when did Mama, little Mama, have that kind of strength? Her skirt had gotten torn, but she didn't care; she just wanted to stand up to those men. The neighbors didn't dare try to stop her, but they didn't take sides with her either. Most of them just stood around tsk-tsking and staring. Finally the men gave Mama an evil look and pushed her away, and while she was gathering herself they bumped their way through the neighbors and ran off into the alley. A taxi was waiting for them and they got away.

It was much later when Mama told me that Brother was dead and that I had better get myself focused and study hard. And that's when Mama started to act strange. She didn't go to the market very often. A lot of the time she'd lie down and complain about how she ached all over. I wonder. . . . What would Mama think . . . if she saw me now? What would she say? "I don't feel heavyhearted anymore"? Or maybe "My heart is all burned up"? After that news arrived, why did Mama go looking around downtown so often? She'd forget to stock her market stall, and early in the morning she'd take out her one and only satin skirt and go downtown. More and more, when I returned from school at dinnertime she'd ignore me and just sit on the edge of the veranda staring into space, all wrapped up in something. I was frightened by Mama at times like that. I was afraid she wanted to get rid of me and run off somewhere. When I tried to shake her out of it, she'd yell at me: "What's the matter with you? You don't have a clue, do you? When are you going to understand? Idiot!" Whenever I passed the neighborhood aunties squatting beside the street and they started tsk-tsking and talking about how it was a good thing I was so dull-witted, or I'd be out looking for my brother, my heart dropped. I'd never felt Brother's dead body with my own hands, so how could I believe he was dead? He was off studying in some distant place, and who knows, maybe he'd come back during vacation.

Mother had stopped going to the market by then. I wonder if she was preparing for something. Chŏng-ja said that Mama went to their place several times and had her grandfather write a big long letter for her. And the few times I had seen her leave for the market, I didn't know if she had some other business to take care of or—the thing I worried about—if she was going off somewhere and leaving me. The scariest thing was when she sat on the edge of the veranda not doing anything. Not looking at me, not crying, but her eyes red all around. It must have been blood that was gathering in her eyes, not tears. I was afraid she'd cry bright red tears. How could she stop going to work at the market? How could we live, how could we save money for Brother?

There I go again—Brother's dead, so Mama doesn't need to save money for him. But is he really dead? What's it like to die? Do you just get holes in you? It must hurt like the devil to die. But then how can the likes of me know how bad it can hurt when I'm *not* dead? Yes, that day I should have drowned myself in the current of people that swept through the city, I should have disappeared forever among the waves of voices, moving bodies, and faces. . . . Those strange, dancing waves, blue furrows sweeping in and out, the faces sinking in those furrows. Mama ran out into those waves. She left me all alone, like she was flicking off a caterpillar, without a single look back at me. I called for her, I yelled. . . . I ran. I was afraid Mama would become a dark speck in the crowd, that she would disappear from me forever and ever. And then what happened? Yes, it was so sudden . . . it happened so quickly—all at once, really . . . the waves moved faster, every which way . . . broke up . . . formed again . . . and then that black curtain. After that I saw nothing. I tried to rip that curtain with my fingernails, but it kept falling over me. It was like a snake wrapping itself around my brain.

Mama started acting strange last fall. The men in suits left an envelope. I wonder what was in it. A letter from Brother to Mama and me? I have to find Brother. But Brother couldn't write a letter to Mama if he was dead, could he? I never wrote to Brother. A voice inside me cried out, big as an open gate, *Brother!* But after I wrote down that one word, there was nothing more to say.

In his letters to us he never failed to include some words for me. The letters arrived once a week, then once a month, and then they grew scarce. Last summer he didn't spend more than three days with us. He said he had a lot of studying to do, and he had to work and earn money. Oh yes, and that sickly yellow color in his face—it was like a plague spirit was inside him. Several of his friends came around . . . and when they left, he didn't go with them. He stayed barely three days. But during those three days he spent hardly any time at home. At daybreak he left for the hills, and he didn't return till dark. It wasn't long before he had disappeared.

I wonder what's become of our house now that no one's there. Chŏng-sun must have gone there several times. How many others went there, then turned around and went back home? Or maybe the whole neighborhood's gone. Maybe nobody came looking for Mama or Brother. Our empty kitchen must feel awfully lonely. The edge of the veranda where I used to doze must be awfully sad. And the veranda floor, its wood so old and shiny—I wonder if it can cry. I wonder where Mama disappeared to. I have to see Brother. I'm not sure, but didn't someone—maybe those men—say he had a burial mound? I have so many things to tell him. But first I have to get this curtain off me. Maybe I can bite through it. I'm so tired. But I have to get it off me, I have to. It was a good thing I left. But why am I so sleepy? I feel so much like sleeping. But if I do I'm in trouble.

I'm thirsty. Always thirsty. And how did I end up not being able to move? If I had some water I think I could start to wake up. No, don't sleep. Maybe I ought to pinch myself. I have to wake up. But I can't feel it when I pinch. I can twist the skin around and there's no mark, see? And now there's no strength left in my fingers. . . . You simply can't go to sleep. . . . You have to see Brother. Even if it's just his grave. He'll be so shocked. If he asks about Mama . . . what will I say? If I tell him I'm the only one left and I came a long way to see him, I'm afraid he'll turn away from me. I wonder if a dead person can get mad. Would he screw up his face and get mad at me for coming all that way? I wonder if he's suffocating there inside his grave. I'm so thirsty! Stay awake. You don't want to get lost on the way. Brother's probably sleeping now. Because it's night.

3

No one knows how she arrived in Okp'o. Several tourists and fishermen recalled seeing a girl along the banks of the Kŭm, but there was no solid evidence that it was in fact her. The particulars we had learned about her were of no help in our search after she left the neighborhood with her mother that day. Nor was the photo the neighbors had obtained for us; whenever we showed it to someone, we were met with a shake of the head.

I guess we found those denials unconvincing. Those who reported seeing a girl remembered only that she was in her early teens and had long hair; if we pressed them further, they would merely say that they hadn't paid special attention to her. Perhaps on that day, terrified by her mother's death, or maybe it was something worse than terror, she had found a place to hide. And who can say what kind of change may have come over her during that time? Hairstyle, clothing, even one's expression—there comes a point when such evidence loses its persuasiveness. If it was her they had seen, then it's safe to say she had been wandering in this vicinity for weeks since that day. Had she, then, appeared in Okp'o after keeping to herself in some unknown place during that time?

There was no one to tell us what she had done during that interval or how she had managed to feed herself. And trying to imagine what she had experienced on her way to Okp'o (experiences she herself probably doesn't remember) was like going down a blind alley. Isn't it still possible for a person to wander the mountains and riversides of our country, if not the large cities, and be offered something to moisten her lips or ease her hunger? It wouldn't have been much of a problem to hide beside a paddy, dry field, or orchard and find herself a few edibles. Doubtless, though, she was preoccupied with matters other than filling her stomach.

We were told that the youngest son of a family named Kang had gone outside to work and had seen her sleeping peacefully against one of the mounds in the family's ancestral burial ground on the outskirts of Naesan Village. He was reluctant to shoo away someone taking refuge among the graves of his ancestors. So he found a place for her as an errand girl in town, at the drinking place managed by the Okp'o woman.

At first she was troublesome, for whenever she saw Kang's son in his reservist's uniform and rubber shoes she attempted to run away to Naesan Village. He had sat her on his cultivator and at least three times on the way into town she had tried to jump off, but she seemed so pitiful he couldn't let her escape, and after a lot of trouble he was finally able to deliver her to the Okp'o woman.

The girl stayed exactly one week. She arrived late in the afternoon, and until late in the evening she dogged the Okp'o woman's heels. That night she came down with a fever and brought back up all she had eaten; the Okp'o woman had fed her too much too soon. The Okp'o woman had a nagging suspicion that something was not right with the girl, and so she dispensed with long-winded explanations about her to others and instead washed her, changed her clothes, then lay down beside her and cradled her head in the crook of her arm until the girl fell asleep. She told us that when dawn arrived she felt such pity for the girl, panting in her sleep, that she patted her back until the fever in her forehead went down. She had asked the girl no questions, and the girl had maintained her silence. When she awakened that morning, her eyes seemed to have no focus. The Okp'o woman could make no sense of this.

Perhaps the girl felt like poking those eyes that saw nothing. Those defenseless arms, that body as useless as a pile of straw, her young age that made it difficult for her to cope—perhaps the girl wanted to rid herself of all these things, cast them aside, curse them. How many times was that still immature body of hers abused by the weight of the nightmares that blanketed her memory even in her hour of deepest sleep? And how can we explain the girl's odd habit, described by the Okp'o woman, of flailing her arms while she slept? Perhaps it was sleep itself that she was fighting. When she awakened, the curtain of sleep was replaced by the murmur of everyday life and the dusty sunlight.

There had probably been a moment when she had forgotten everything. But then something insignificant—a soft sound, a vague face, a smell, a momentary silence—would cause her to bolt out of bed or throw her into a quandary that paralyzed her. It always involved her mother; something had happened to her mother. And it always produced an intense suffering.

That suffering pulsed with the suppressed memories of myriad faces and a lightning chain of events. Screaming faces. Faces falling to the ground. Menacing, assaulting faces. Bloody faces. Denuded faces. Faces twitching like fish out of water. Faces that disappeared silently. Faces pursued. Glaring faces. Shouting faces and arms waving wildly. Common faces, forever hardened. Smashed faces. Faceless faces.

Profiles moving forward. Faces with beautiful, shining foreheads. Faces that combine dreams and power. Faces falling sideways. Faces falling backward to the ground. Faces smashed again.

A face with unseeing eyes that was about to call her name.

The Okp'o woman said she noticed the girl's suppressed sobs, the shoulders heaving silently, the eyes vacant, devoid of tears. Perhaps her memories of that riot of faces had dissolved in her blood, becoming a burdensome, enforced presence that wore her down.

The Okp'o woman asked little of the girl. And the girl did as she was asked. She took the dishes the Okp'o woman handed her, cleaned the floor when it was messy, filled the serving kettles, washed the dishes. A week passed with no particular problem. Maybe five times at most, she dropped a bowl of soup or broke a small dish. From what the Okp'o woman could gather during that week, the girl was by herself and was looking for one of her relatives, who lived someplace distant. On the sixth day the Okp'o woman saw the girl standing at the door, gazing outside, spellbound. There had been a passing rain shower during the day, and that night, ignoring the calls of customers, holding the plates of food the Okp'o woman had given her, the girl stared at the play of light in a mud puddle. The following afternoon, when the Okp'o woman heard the boisterous sounds of a group of young men on the road to the marketplace, the girl was gone. Apart from the cloth bundle she had brought with her, all that was missing was a small amount of money and the clothes given her by the Okp'o woman.

The Okp'o woman had asked her what was in the bundle.

"It was so dirty, but she wouldn't let go of it for days, and she wouldn't tell me what was inside. I told her it was filthy and I'd wash it for her, but no ma'am, she was an obstinate one. Finally I looked inside it while she was asleep. It was a going-out dress, a reddish purple color. It looked like she'd tried to wash it, but it still had bloodstains and dirt on it. I never consciously told myself that something awful had happened to that girl, or that maybe she'd done something awful. But I had a hunch. Anyway, I took out the dress and washed it, I hung it up by the stove, and I ironed it real nice. Then I put it up on the shelf. But I doubt she even noticed it. Not in the state she was in. She was out of it, completely gone. I stuck a couple of bills in the folds of the dress, but I didn't have a chance to tell her that, and then she took off. Her mind was somewhere else, like she was haunted by some monster, and she was keeping it all inside. Tell me, did she find that relative she said she was looking for?"

The Okp'o woman said she didn't know what the girl had seen on the road to the marketplace to make her run off so suddenly. The girl herself probably didn't know.

The young men passing by on the road to the marketplace that day were workers, nine of them. They were on their way to a construction site in Changhang, the Okp'o woman said. But not one of them claimed to have seen the girl. And none of the bus girls on any of the buses leaving Okp'o at the time of her disappearance remembered seeing a girl in a brown cotton skirt and a navy-blue T-shirt. That the girl had regained a normal appearance during her week-long stay at the Okp'o woman's restaurant necessarily threw up an obstacle to our efforts to trace her. How long would it take till onlookers were once again brought to a halt by the sight of her, clothing muddy and wet, face and body filthy, hair disheveled and snarled?

There are times when the lines and the points on a map create an optical illusion. The lines that seem to connect one point with another so systematically prove to be indistinct and unstable, a trap. A single point can extend in countless directions. And we had no reliable coordinates from which to guess which of the many possible lines the girl had taken from Okp'o. She could have gone back the way she had come or continued on; she could have gone in an unknown direction, or she might be going in circles.

Because of this uncertainty, we had to invent a nonlinear itinerary and survey the entire region. To grasp the wanderings of the girl's spirit, for which language had ceased to function, we had to rely on a complex logic. To pinpoint her peculiar journey we had to enter inside of her, remain with her, follow the dictates of her mind. This required a great deal of time, and at every step of the way she distanced herself from us.

The traces she left grew correspondingly and hopelessly faint.

But like wounds that never heal, thoughts of the dear friend who had left us behind, thoughts of the traces left by his little sister, reminded us always of our torpor. Those thoughts were our only map.

4

My eyes are full of sand and my insides are rotting. I'm sure of it. I'm going blind because of that sand. I can hear my eyelids scratching against it when I try to open my eyes. Don't let me go blind. Who's going to recognize me if I can't even recognize myself?

What a weird dream! It's made me wide awake. Why do I feel light after such a heavy sleep?

Somebody dumped me in a village. I didn't see his face, but I felt two strong hands lift me by the waist from behind and toss me on a corner in a village I'd never seen before. I'm not sure why, but I wanted to say thanks. But when I turned my sore body around and looked, no one was there. It was daytime, but off in the distance a mountain started moving very slowly and everything in that direction turned dark. It's strange, I know, but I wasn't afraid. Maybe I was dreaming.

I could still feel the warmth of those hands that had grabbed me around the waist when suddenly people from the village started appearing. They surrounded me where I was lying, and the first thing they said was to tell them everything I'd seen, or else. . . . I wanted to get up, but someone held me down with his foot. "You won't move an inch unless you talk." And then they all took it up like a chorus: "You won't move an inch unless you talk." But I kept my mouth shut and told myself, "It's only a dream—all you have to do is open your eyes." But my eyes were full of sand; they felt so scratchy.

I don't know how I managed to escape. I was running up a hill and I saw some black dots off in the distance that looked like they were moving. They grew into beetles that were big as toads, disgusting things, and when I saw them crawling up behind me I tried to run faster. I knew there was a cave at the top of the hill, so I ran and ran till I got there. How did I know the cave was there? Dreams really are weird. As I went inside, I heard a horrible noise. The beetles were knee-high by now and they were having a hard time moving their six bristly legs, but they were marching single file toward the mouth of the cave. Those oily black eyes, those stinking shells, those throbbing chests with the white lines showing—they were awful!

Quickly I broke off some pieces of rock from the wall of the cave. Once I was in the cave I felt a strength I couldn't've imagined, and with just the palm of my hand and a little effort those pieces of rock came right off the wall. One by one I took aim at those monsters, between the eyes or on the chest, and knocked them down with the rocks. It was like something in a comic book. Those beetles were flipped over on their backs with their disgusting legs kicking frantically in the air—except for one that made it to the mouth of the cave and stuck its head inside. I picked up a rock so big it made my arms ache and smashed it down on the bug over and over. I was so scared I couldn't open my eyes. To keep that horrible smashed head and those slimy feelers from covering me, I went way back inside the cave and lay down, held my breath, and waited. . . .

What if I told this dream to Sun-shik's grandmother? I bet she'd say it was a bad sign. But there's nothing to be afraid of now. And nothing to hope for. Not for a girl like me, who's lost everything. If I could just cry my eyes out. But I can't— I'm all dried up inside.

Yes, there were hands that dropped me in some bushes in the middle of the night. Big, hard hands that picked me up from behind while I was sleeping and dropped me in some bushes where no one could see. When I came to and managed to stand up and was struggling to turn around, I heard a car going away in the distance. No, I wasn't sleeping; I'd blacked out. The moment I saw the ruined body of my mother and her face all twisted up as she tried to call my name, that heavy black curtain fell over my eyes. At that moment, the moment Mama fell, I could no longer see past or present. I should have removed that curtain, should have ripped it open even if it meant the death of me too. But instead I fainted—what an idiot! How will I be able to see Mama? Part of that curtain's still there.

How long was I lying there covered by the curtain? How many people passed by, walking right over me? When I came to, I couldn't budge—it felt like a dresser had fallen on me. My back hurt all over, like someone was hammering on it. I thought it was broken. I started crying, not because it hurt, but because I was so sure it was broken. See how stupid you were? What a silly girl! No wonder people made fun of you and cussed you out.

It was night, black night. The air was damp and chilly— I could feel it in my bones. I wanted to dig myself into the ground, but every time I moved, I was afraid my bones would scream and snap, so I decided to put up with the cold. I looked up just enough to see around me; not a single light. I kept my eyes open; otherwise I'd see those monsters again. In the darkness the hills looked like they were collapsing.

When was it—last year? the year before that?—when Mama bought me that going-out dress? I was afraid that it would get damp, that mixed in with the dampness was a filthy secret hidden in the ground, a stain I'd never be able to get rid of. But that worry of mine was nothing. And so was the ache in my back. Because a feeling thousands, no, millions of times more frightening was slowly settling into my bones, spreading like poison, bringing my sleepy nerves back to life. And so, though my back felt like it would give out, I shot to my feet, looked around, and croaked like a crow.

Clouds covered the moonless sky like the huge wings of a scavenging bird. Among them were a few stars, twinkling painfully, spots of pus from a sore, bringing goose bumps to the back of my neck.

Daylight would come somewhere. Over there, where the spooky shadows of that tree were jittering about. No, that way, where nothing blocked my view, where the land of the goblins was being sucked into utter darkness. Or maybe the other direction, from that mountain that made me afraid my heart would crack if I looked at it just once, that mountain approaching me, trampling everything in its path, that massive mountain, crawling, sliding toward me.

No, dawn would come instead where there wasn't a mountain blocking the way, from where that road stretched far out into the distance. No life, no movement. Except for earthworms, grasshoppers, things like that . . . or maybe poisonous snakes, boa constrictors. How long was I sitting there, holding my breath, afraid to pat down my goose bumps? And who had brought me there?

Suddenly insects from the grass were calling out in every direction like hungry ghosts. It sounded like they were calling inside my ears and it made me dizzy. That's when I stopped holding my breath and wailed: "Insects, you insects, save me!"

My voice echoed against the mountain. I wailed until dawn approached—it came from the end of that dirt road, just like I'd expected. Two words surged up my throat—"Mama!" "Brother!"—but I swallowed them so hard my lower back ached.

I couldn't call out those words. No more sitting beneath that dark mountain! No more crying and calling out! Understand? That's enough crying. I cried too much, and in the space of a single night I shriveled and aged. And now nobody can recognize me. If I saw the neighbors now they'd walk right by; they wouldn't know me. I wonder if Mama and Brother would know me. Yes, they would—regardless of the spots on my face, my injuries, my wrinkles—because we resemble one another.

I got old all at once. And those two words I can't call out are buried deep inside me. I'm alone, all alone. Because I couldn't get rid of that curtain. But who was it that loaded me into a car when I blacked out and then left me at the foot of that dark mountain? Was it someone who knew me? I must have seen dozens of people on the road—was he one of them?

Yes, I cried till daybreak, cried my eyes out. I cried, terrified by the darkness. My crying mixed with the calls of the insects and I cried even louder, afraid I'd grow feelers and sprout green wings from my armpits. I followed the road in the direction of dawn. And for the first time I saw the bluish tint of that road. I didn't look back; I was afraid the darkness was chasing me. And I made up my mind to find my brother. A voice inside my head was whispering to me, encouraging me to go straight down that road; it would take me to where my brother was lying, waiting for me. I forgot the creaking of my body, my sprained ankles, my messed-up

hair, and watched the whole wide universe open up in front
of me. I would have to wander that universe.

How scared and lonely Brother must be, locked up in
darkness. He's waiting for someone to tell him about Mama
and me. But what should I tell him if he asks *me*? How can I
explain to him the damage to my body? Well, I still have a
little time. But how can I tell him about that black curtain,
about Mama and me, about that day, without breaking
down?

If my brother says okay, we'll go back to our neighborhood.
Maybe they're keeping the lights on at night. Maybe they're
waiting, wide awake, clubs in their hands. No, I can't do it. I
can't go home under that bright light, even if my brother
wants to. I can't tell him about that black curtain. I just can't.
What if sadness has turned his dead body into powder and
there's nothing left of him anymore? . . . It's too late for me to
feel sorry that I left that day.

The dawn turned more and more blue, spreading down
the road, drawing me, and I started walking that road. This
was the light I had waited for all night, but when it wrapped
itself gently around me I felt guilty, scared. Where was I? It
was a damp dirt road and on the far side was a thin layer of
fog. Through that fog I thought I could see people. Two or
three of them seemed to be coming toward me, and I could
make out the shape of something they were carrying on their
backs. . . . I couldn't take another step. I was too frightened to
find out what was moving toward me, and I shut my eyes.
This wasn't the fog I used to see in our neighborhood. I had
never seen such fog, such a strange dawn. I had to get away
and hide, but I couldn't move. Finally, with my eyes closed, I
struggled across the paddies, falling off the raised paths a couple of times, until I could feel thorns scratching low down on

my legs. If only it were night, so I could walk and walk and never be seen by others.

There had to be paths in those mountains. And things to eat too. When had I eaten last? Hiding in bushes at the foot of the mountains, I gazed at the emerald paddies. No sign of life anywhere.

Hunger clawed at my insides like the sharp teeth of a rake. It had been a long time since my stomach had grumbled. Poor innards, all dried up! I had to find running water and moisten them.

I was lucky. I found petals to eat, shoots, every once in a while a piece of unripe fruit, and very rarely some cabbage roots or a sweet potato. One day I devoured some pink petals and bush clover shoots and threw it all back up. But the very next day I was up and down the slopes looking for more flowers to eat.

I walked for days, deep in the mountains, always watching my shadow appear on my left and shrink toward the right. At night I found valleys sheltered from the wind and slept beneath a blanket of branches. When I closed my eyes I saw spring green turn to gray, and gray to navy blue, and then I seemed to evaporate—I was sucked, swiftly and silently, into the far distance. And that's when I saw my mother. And sometimes Brother too.

On the third day—or was it the fifth?—I woke up to find my brother looking at me with a smile. "Brother!" But then his face disappeared and in its place was the face of a man looking right at me. His hair was cut square and there were moles on his face. Motioning to me not to be scared, he took a mesh bag that was slung over his shoulder and tossed it to the ground, and then a weird screech came out of his mouth. I shut my eyes again, and when I opened them the man held out two steamed potatoes to me. All my fear melted away and the very next second I had gobbled the potatoes. The man was a mute. He had fishing gear. I felt like those dark moles on his face were covering my heart with shade. The man proceeded to find me some water from a stream.

The next day the mute brought more food—thick pumpkin soup and steamed corn. My gagging went away and I got hiccups instead. Once they started they kept up for a while. The man patted my back, but the hiccups continued. I'd been so long without food, and now my innards were stirring. He brought food on the third day too. And some old clothes. For the first time I inspected my clothes, my pretty clothes. They were so mud-stained I hardly recognized them. I could understand what the man was trying to tell me. It wasn't the first time I'd talked with a mute. A long time ago a mute lived in our neighborhood. Uncle Chang-son, we called him. He had some land, and he married a woman who had her eye on that land. She sold the paddies behind his back and ran away. He lost everything, and he had to pay the woman's debts. He ended up going from door to door doing any kind of physical labor he could. Two years ago Uncle Chang-son left. He said he was going to Seoul. When I was in grade school he'd bought me a pencil case. I never heard a sound from his mouth, but this man here made a weird screech whenever he wanted to say something. He handed me the clothes. He indicated that he wanted me to change, and that he would wash my clothes. He kept his eyes on me all the time I was changing.

The stains were still there after he washed the dress. It needs a good soaping, and the day will come when I'll give it one. I can't lose those clothes. If my mama and brother can't recognize me because my face is wrinkled and I'm scarred all over, I'll take out my clothes and show them. They'll know who I am then, because they bought me those clothes for the Harvest Moon Festival.

The mute hung my clothes on a branch, then lay down beside me and proceeded to stroke my legs and belly for a long time. He kept opening his mouth to say something, but all that came out was that weird sound. He kept struggling like that for a while, and finally ended up making a croaking sound. Instead of words, huge tears fell from his eyes. It was amazing. I looked into his face. I was just like Mama: no more tears came out of my eyes anymore. Sometimes Mama acted like the mute: all she did was croak and pound her chest.

Evening came. The mute had been lying beside me the whole time, stroking my hair and picking off the straw and grass that was sticking to my throat. It happened so fast. Right before nightfall, just as I was falling asleep, a bluebird came between my legs and entered me.

When it was dark the mute picked up his bag and quickly disappeared down the mountain. Before he left, he indicated I should stay where I was and he'd bring food the next day. My eyes were heavy, and in the dense darkness his movements and the swaying of the trees were one big tangle of motion.

It was then that I realized I was slowly turning into a stone. I found I was holding pebbles in each of my hands. And then I seemed vaguely to understand, like the fuzzy outlines of a bad dream I couldn't remember, why that bluebird was pecking inside me.

Maybe it was all an illusion. I've never been able to understand anything. The more I try to force things into my head, the more complicated they seem. It's like a million pieces of string all wrapped up inside my little head—soon they're tangled and then they're hard as a lump of coal. When that bluebird forced itself inside me it hurt badly, but I didn't make a sound. That kind of thing is nothing to me now. Thousands of those birds could attack me, but I'll never cry out, I'll never get down on my knees, I'll never ask for mercy.

That day, the day I blacked out, I lost forty, fifty, a hundred years of my life. That day, when the black curtain draped my memory and the image of my mother's arrested motions—her mouth open in pain, her arms aloft in shock and then floating down like wings to try to cover the holes in her belly—on that day I lost everything forever. When I woke up in the shadow of the mountain that night, I didn't know. I didn't know that in a single instant I had undergone a terrible change. If someone cheated or insulted my mother, she would say, "You'll see, tomorrow I'll be a completely different person, and if you try to pull that on me again you'll pay for it!" And then like an idiot, off she'd go to the market the next day with the very same people, chattering away as if nothing had happened.

Mother turned strange and didn't realize it. People said her soul had left her. I wasn't sure what they meant by that. I had a notion that a bizarre spirit was living inside her. She walked much faster than she ever had before, mouth clamped shut, eyes dry, a red flush to her tanned cheeks, head erect, eyes gazing off into the distance. Once I came across her talking with the neighbors. She went on for over an hour, and I was amazed at how well she expressed herself. What was really strange was that she wanted to dictate letters to me, letters whose contents I didn't understand, and she asked me, the stutterer, to read things written down on paper. By that time I wouldn't have been surprised if she had somehow learned to write overnight. And maybe if the mute were in her place he could suddenly learn to talk.

And for a moment that night it seemed a few words would spill out of the mute. He had asked me to wait for him till the next day, but I didn't. It grew darker, and when my eyes got used to it I decided to go down the mountain. I took the bundle the mute had packed for me and followed the ridge crest down. When the path came to an end I wandered until I found another, and I followed that one to the end. I came out into fields, and where the fields ended a river stretched out in the distance. I came across a village and to avoid it I went back up in the mountains. But I got so hungry I could hardly walk, and I had to come down. And finally I encountered people. More and more I would forget why I was walking. I stopped thinking about where I was going, and like someone in a trance I took whatever those people offered me, including a place to stay for a night, two nights, or longer. When they left, I left. And until I reached the river, I sometimes ran, sometimes rested, all the while with the sensation that the nearer I came to it, the farther it receded.

Finally, there it was in front of me. Suddenly I thought of the ocean. I began to feel that it was the ocean I had left home to see. And so I followed the river, I followed its current. But then everything grew vague and I felt I would never reach the ocean. And there came a time when I woke up to a rain shower on the riverside and remembered why I had left that day.

Along the river I met more people than I can count. Men and women who fled at my approach, children who grabbed my long streams of hair from behind and giggled. Dogs didn't bother to chase me, but just barked and bared their teeth. I remember a day when it began to rain. I rested at the deserted riverside, hoping I could somehow dissolve in the water. But later in the day when the skies cleared and my body was still there, the only thing I could do was haul myself to my feet.

And along the river more birds entered me with their sharp beaks. There must have been dozens of them inside me, each in its nest. If I kept still and closed my eyes I could hear them chirping, and I would start trembling. What did they want? Freedom? Their provider? If only I could give them what they wanted! I opened my mouth so wide my jaws hurt, I gagged, I struggled to get those birds out, but not one of them flew out, unless it was while I slept.

The day came when I forgot about the ocean. I crossed the river in a boat. And for the first time, there on the other side, I looked back. I realized I'd reached the point of no return. A yellow cloud drifted over the woods on the other side and then everything—the woods, the riverside, the water—was engulfed in flames. Who had set the fire? And who had cast that shower of flames before my eyes? Then I saw people thronging across the river of fire, shouting, arms flailing at me. I had to get away from them. And that meant that for a long time I forgot what I had to do.

I can never go back across that river. Never. Unless I find my brother. As I crossed the river, all of those faces, those sad faces that concealed something explosive, they all dissolved in the water. Those who beat me, those who gave me food and a place to sleep, those who felt my forehead and gave me medicine, those who stuck a bluebird inside me and then ran away—river, those faces belong to you now! Receive them. Because I have no strength; my mind has no place for them. Someday I'll return, when the black curtain lifts and I can love myself without reservation. Keep them until that day. Thank you, my friend. Until we meet again, take care.

5

No longer did the man force alcohol down the girl; no longer did his blind, incomprehensible rage provoke assaults on her. The more he had abused her, the more miserable he had felt the next day. His slapping, instead of producing a change in her behavior, had merely drained his energy.

When he returned in the evening to his shedlike dwelling he always found her sitting exactly where he had left her. Occasionally the place had been tidied up and the dirty dishes scrubbed clean. The man began to bring home groceries, and upon his arrival the girl, without prompting, mechanically dusted herself off and rose. She lit the kerosene stove at the side of the room, cooked rice, and made stew. In complete silence they placed the meal tray between them and ate. Half in disgust and half in fascination, the man sometimes observed the face of this distracted girl as she hunched over like a worm and slowly chewed her rice as if she were counting the grains inside her mouth. The more carefully he watched, the more awkward he felt: her expression was too impassive for someone her age, difficult as that was to determine in the first place. It was the expression of someone who had lived out her youth. What had caused such a disfigurement?

But before he could ask her that, he was struck by the thought that perhaps he was partly to blame. When he looked at her in that light, he found it more difficult to persuade himself, despite that idiotic smile of hers, that something in her mind had stopped working. For perhaps she lived quite normally in a world unknown to him, a mental landscape beyond his grasp. Maybe it was his ignorance that made her seem strange; perhaps in her eyes he was equally peculiar. Then again, he wondered if she even had the capacity for thought.

The man had seen a number of crazed people lingering in the dark spaces of the city. Most of the faces were similar, and they provoked in him sometimes indifference, sometimes ridicule. Those faces now reappeared in his mind, accompanied by a question mark. There on the face of the girl, as she chewed her food carefully, like someone who had bitten a piece of grit, were superimposed all those lunatic faces he had seen, and in an instant the girl's face seemed to shrivel up. As if afraid that her wrinkled flesh would disintegrate, he reached out and propped up her chin.

"Eat up. You need to get your energy back."

The tenderness of his voice surprised him. With a shake of his head he tried to dispel the disturbing image he had just entertained, but he found himself unable to release the girl's chin. A hot storm of emotion blew through him, searing his innards into shriveled knots. He tried to conceal the sensation:

"I'm sorry, girl. Really I am."

Seeing the man's reddening eyes, the girl burst into laughter, her gaping mouth spewing bits of rice onto the tray. The man joined in, laughing until his shoulders heaved. He wanted to identify with her, to enter her and repair what was broken inside her.

One day the man told one of the other men at the construction site that he felt he'd been infected. He was sure it was the plague, and he asked, half in jest, if such diseases still existed. But then he told the other to be sure to keep his distance.

At times the man stayed out almost till dawn, drinking and playing cards, then stole home while the girl was sprawled out asleep. Then a dreadful anxiety would envelop him; he would tell himself he must put an end to it, this relationship he had entered into in spite of himself. If only she would disappear! And if his drunken gaze failed to locate her rag-doll form in the darkness, his mind would clear instantly and he would frantically grope for her. Not until he found her stick-like arms would his panicked breathing subside. And when in her sleep she responded to his ungentle hand with a faint, animal-like moan, he would pat her as if she were a baby.

"There now. It's all right. Sleep to your heart's content."

The best times were when she slept. At least then there were no strange outcries, no incongruous giggling. If she happened to murmur a few words the way a normal person might, he said "Yes?" and waited expectantly for an answer, as if the two of them might actually have a conversation. And sometimes, just for the sake of a brief exchange that wasn't necessarily relevant to anything, he would squat beside her and wait for her to mumble something about one of her dreams.

It seemed for the most part that her dreams were peaceful. In the dark the man could make out the fleeting smiles, addressed to who knows whom, that brightened her pitiful face with its chapped cheeks. Hoping a solution to her situation might emerge from her dreams, he would gently prod her and strain to listen, as if consulting an oracle.

"What are you dreaming about? You can tell me, it's all right."

Her only response to these whispers was to scratch her ear before lapsing back into a deep sleep.

At length he stopped putting fruitless questions to her, whether they arose from curiosity or from his fear of what he might have done to her. He no longer threatened or coaxed her. Not that he had grown indifferent; rather, he was compelled to concentrate on fathoming the reasons this girl had been driven to the brink of insanity. But it was all in vain. Every scenario he considered became less plausible when he observed her face. He might detect a pronounced color there, some frightful incident, but whatever it was far surpassed the limited bounds of his imagination, and before he could even begin to identify it his head would be wracked with pain and he would have to suspend his thinking, afraid it was not some horrible incident but he himself who was the primary cause of her condition.

He could no longer tell how long it had been since he had become incapable of forcing alcohol down her, abusing her, invading her body. Instead a different series of questions rose before him: *Does she even recognize me? Can she tell me apart from others? Is it me she's smiling at? Or is it a face that's stuck in her messed-up mind? Did she think I was someone else when she started following me at the riverside a couple of months ago?*

Desperately the man searched her blank gaze for the slightest glimmer of recognition. He bought her a pair of shoes, clothes, a hairbrush. Her response to each of these items was a laugh that he could only characterize as the color red, a laugh that sent a lingering chill down his spine.

6

We were wrong. We had thought she would go in the direction of Changhang, toward the sea. All we could do was return to Okp'o and start over again from the drinking place where she had stayed. Okp'o made a good base because there were only a few areas she could have reached from there by bus. We realized she could very well have recrossed the river, intending to return home, but in the end we limited ourselves to the possibility that she had remained among the towns on this side. For some reason we couldn't imagine her going back across the river.

We will be eternally grateful to the Okp'o woman. She was much more systematic than we were in following up on any leads regarding the girl. Who else but she would have brought us together with Im, a man who drove a delivery truck between

Okp'o and Sŏch'ŏn? On one of his trips to Sŏch'ŏn Im had seen someone corresponding to the description of the girl given by the Okp'o woman. And there was more: Im had noticed the girl in the company of a man named Kim Sang-t'ae who was walking his bicycle along the road. This man Kim was the nephew of an unprepossessingly wealthy man in Sŏch'ŏn.

Im, though, was reluctant to tell us more than what he had told the Okp'o woman. He asked who we were and why we were looking for the girl, said he didn't know where we could find Kim Sang-t'ae, and allowed that the girl he had seen might have been someone else. In order to reassure him we had to embroider. The Okp'o woman joined in the subterfuge, detaining Im with drinks and snacks and telling him that the girl was a distant relative of hers. Ultimately Im saw fit to give us a general impression of Kim Sang-t'ae's appearance and a rough idea of where he lived. With this information, and after promising the Okp'o woman we would notify her at some point in the future, we boarded a bus for Sŏch'ŏn.

Rain swept in that afternoon, and as we lurched along in the rear of the bus the fields outside seemed miraculously fertile, the mountains bluer behind their veil of moisture. The sheets of rain fell evenly over the innocent landscape, lashing the ground painlessly, a tender tattoo that left no deep scars. The rickety bus lurched violently and the passengers pitched and swayed, silent and uncomplaining as puppets. We gazed at the rain-soaked road, each of us revisiting our numerous nightmarish memories.

Suddenly one among us gave a long, falling sigh and his shoulders began heaving uncontrollably. We allowed his sobs to play out to the end as we knew they must, though it seemed he would choke if they continued long enough. It was as if the excruciating pain we all felt had erupted through him alone. The way to Sŏch'ŏn was long, or at least it felt long, and it was our good fortune that none of the other passengers paid attention to us.

It did not prove difficult to find Kim Sang-t'ae with his long, pale face that suggested he was in his mid-twenties. We learned that he had dropped out of school because of his health and for the last three years had lived on the proceeds of real estate obtained with the help of his family. He was a gloomy man who seemed reluctant to talk. He did tell us that he managed a sporting goods shop, but his real source of income was a building he rented out in Taech'ŏn. He seemed sensitive to the point of nervous instability.

Kim was noticeably startled when we mentioned the girl, and he promptly clamped his mouth shut. But he didn't seem to be hiding anything. Instead, his expression seemed to say that nothing worth mentioning had happened in the first place. It would take time, we realized, to draw him out of his shell. And so we sat in silence, listening to the whine of the fan in the nearly empty tearoom, and before long we had lapsed into thoughts of our own.

Eventually our instincts told us it was best to speak straightforwardly, and we began to explain the reasons we had been looking for the girl since May, following the events in that city to the south. He nodded and said simply that we didn't have to waste our breath; he had already figured out the story in broad outline. We then described how we had found him. Expectantly we awaited his response. What we got, each of us in turn, was a sardonic smile that seemed to say, "Well, you know all about me now—what more do you want?"

After a long silence he asked if we believed what Im, the truck driver, had said. This puzzled us. Im, we explained, had given us only the most cursory information. Evidently there was something we hadn't been told, and this realization gnawed at us. Looking at Kim, we began to wonder if the girl had been in this town and if during her stay something irrevocable had happened to her. We felt we had no more time to waste. This lack of patience is the critical weakness of youth. We were all in the habit of hoping for the quickest, most favorable outcome, and though we realized that this inclination led to more mistakes on our part, we were far from convinced of the wisdom of indirection or mere waiting.

Kim seemed to sense that we were prepared to browbeat him if we had to, and finally he said in a reassuring tone that the girl had probably found herself a safe place. He then took us to the abandoned farm on the outskirts of town where he had found her. The land all around was overgrown with a forest of weeds. Some time ago, he explained, a customer at the sporting goods shop had told him a strange story: for an uncertain period of time a girl had been living at that farm, and many a man from Sŏch'ŏn had gone there to violate her, apparently with impunity. The girl charged nothing for her services and was fair game for all who visited. Several versions of the story made the rounds: she was a sweet young thing; or she was just a kid; or she was a bit older and ripe for the plucking. She'd been kicked out by her husband and in-laws; she was a prostitute who had escaped from a red-light district; or else she was simply a madwoman. Despite all these rumors, Kim had never spoken with anyone who had actually been to this farm where the woman was secluded.

But then there was a direct sighting. The errand boy at Kim's shop, on his way home from a delivery, had seen a girl near that farm foraging frantically for weeds and grasses whose edges looked sharp enough to slice your palm. That night Kim found himself driving there.

At this point Kim looked defiantly at us, one dubious but attentive face after another, then gave us a dismissive wave— "I know what you're thinking!" he seemed to be saying. With that he began another story, apparently unrelated to the girl we were seeking.

He had had a sweetheart, a neighbor girl he used to carry around piggyback, who had died before reaching adulthood. The neighbors had carried on about the difference in their ages, and everyone blamed him for her death. Girls ran away at the sight of him, convinced he harbored a grudge against those the same age as his sweetheart and would infect them with a fatal disease. Life without her was hell at first, he said. But then as time went by her image, instead of fading, grew ever more vivid inside him, and now she was a cherished presence in the innermost recesses of his heart. "I'm never alone," he declared, caressing his chest. We then realized why Im had said there was something chronically wrong with Kim.

The rumors of the girl on the farm reminded Kim of how he had been victimized, and he decided that by rescuing the vagabond girl he could put to rest the lies of his neighbors that he wrought harm on his dead sweetheart's age-mates.

We could not conceal our impatience. Our sense of urgency prevented us from being swept up in Kim's sentimentality. At the same time, by swallowing our questions we in effect had submitted to the silent lash of his digression.

Kim had waited for an hour at a distance from the hutlike farmhouse, wondering if the girl had a visitor. When finally he had gone inside, the glare of his flashlight revealed the girl lying motionless on the dirt floor. At that instant, for the first time in his life, he felt shame and fear at the sight of another human being.

At this point in his narrative one of us produced for Kim the photo of the girl that we had displayed to countless people in the hope of a positive identification. A hint of surprise appeared in his eyes, but then they grew still and he studied the photo intently. Slowly he shook his head. Someone pounded once on the table. It was hopeless! We were back at square one.

"This wasn't the face I saw, I'm sure of it. But if her situation has improved since then, I suppose this could be her. I don't know when this was taken, but it's awful to think I can barely recognize her."

Her physical condition was even worse than rumored, Kim told us. She must have gone without nourishment for days, weeks even. She seemed comatose, only feeble movements of her limbs indicating she was alive. She smelled awful and her body was covered with bruises.

Some ten days must have passed between the time she had left the Okp'o woman and her arrival in Sŏch'ŏn. By then she had been wandering almost six weeks.

That night Kim had the girl admitted to a clinic. Unfortunately he was seen loading her into his vehicle, and subsequent comments by medical personnel gave rise to a bizarre rumor: the spirit of Kim's dead sweetheart had returned, intent on revenge. It seems rumors are like odors: the more pungent they are, the faster they spread. By the next day the rumor had been magnified and was circulating recklessly among the people of Sŏch'ŏn. This particular fabrication was even uglier than the ones that had tormented Kim for so long.

People gathered at the entrance to the clinic. Rocks were thrown through the window of the girl's sickroom. Four days later a delegation of local people confronted the clinic director and demanded that he turn her out. They claimed the girl was unclean and possessed by a male spirit.

That night Kim laid the girl in his car and drove her to Taech'ŏn. She began to rave. She spoke in fragments, disconnected words, struggling in the confines of the car, gasping through her gaping mouth: "Dead—brother—black—holes, red holes. . . ." These words burst out again and again. But without a context, they made no sense to him.

At the clinic in Taech'ŏn the girl must have briefly recovered her senses. Waking up and seeing Kim's unfamiliar face, she had flinched. In spite of her youth, dark circles had formed around her eyes. If memory served him correctly, Kim said, that was the first intelligible expression he had noticed since removing her from the farm. But it was an expression of fear, and that pained him. Kim tried to reassure her, but her eyes burned with distrust. He sat beside her bed nevertheless, for her defensiveness involved no danger; it was no different from an inadvertent mistake, a random remnant of an emotion not yet extinguished.

Hers was a face aged by something too great and profound for her years. That face now focused on Kim's, a gloomy face that had gradually sunk into a pent-up swirl of suffering, a face grown twisted over the years.

The strange thing was, her sun-darkened hand, shriveled and hard like wire, took hold of Kim's where it rested on the bedside. Presently Kim began talking to her, his painful history spilling out like water through a sluice gate, a history he had stuffed deep inside himself, away from others. Kim wondered if she was even listening. And if so, did she understand?

Probably she did. But even if she hadn't paid attention to his account, she must have, the instant her hand reached out for his, understood the depth of his suffering. Or perhaps for her by then, everyone's history was extra baggage. For suffering can't be categorized, it has no distinctive coloration. Perhaps all suffering follows the same course. Once on that course, people's histories can't help coloring each other, the suffering differentiated only by intensity. Mutual recognition becomes inevitable.

This man Kim, so much older than the girl, rested his forehead on the humble clinic bed, shoulders heaving as he told his story. Before he was done she was once again asleep.

When she awoke, her face was expressionless—no fear, no defensiveness. The hand that had reached out to Kim before was now gathered close. She fell into a pattern of pinching her arms, her shoulders, her thighs. She pinched herself all over, as if to keep from falling asleep as long as she still possessed a thread of consciousness. Or perhaps she needed reassurance that her physical self still existed. With every pinch the lids of her hazy eyes slowly fluttered, like the flickering of a loosely screwed-in light bulb on a windy day.

From time to time her cadaverous face lifted and a smile escaped. It seemed she confused his face with another, for sometimes she opened her mouth as if to address him.

One day Kim ventured a few questions in a confidential tone: What was her name? Where was her home? Where was she going? In an equally confidential tone, and looking directly at Kim, the girl replied only that her mother had died with holes in her and that she was going to Seoul to look for her brother. The rest of his questions she didn't seem to understand.

Several days passed with the girl seemingly indifferent to where she now found herself. Half of the food she took in was vomited back up, half stayed down. According to the doctor, her internal organs were compromised and would require long-term treatment. And some of her body systems had been damaged beyond repair. Traces of gross contusions were evident up and down her back. It was a wonder, the doctor said, that she had endured so long in such a condition. A general hospital could provide a more detailed prognosis, he added. Most of her damaged organs wouldn't show an improvement during the week she spent in this private clinic in Taech'ŏn; her injuries were too severe for a quick recovery.

The most singular thing was how quickly the girl's digestive system returned to normal. To Kim and the doctor, who could imagine how long the girl had gone hungry, this seemed miraculous. We, however, found it perfectly reasonable. To endure the physically shattering shock the girl must have suffered, one needed the life force of a weed. One's innards had to be tough enough to digest nails. They had to be hardened enough not to break down even if empty for days. If we speak of a miracle, shouldn't it be the girl's life itself, vestiges of which we had found?

When we left to look for the girl, after learning too late, much too late, that her mother was no longer of this world, we clung hopefully to precisely this renewing potential of the weedlike life force. The girl, we now knew, was much tougher in body than in soul.

Even if the girl's consciousness plunged now and then into a dungeonlike oblivion of chaos and derangement, her body accomplished its most basic functions. Instinctively it followed the sun; her feet automatically avoided pitfalls, moving with certainty toward that which would satisfy her hunger. Somewhere inside of her was inscribed the record of what had happened to her, and even when she mistook utter strangers for her kin, even when she confused past with present, her senses led her on a course more certain than rationality.

On her eighth day in Taech'ŏn she flung aside her covers like a corpse removing its shroud and rose. She picked up her bundle from beside the head of the bed and walked straight for the door. The nurse tried to detain her while she contacted Kim, but by the time he arrived the girl had escaped. She must have walked quickly, eyes ahead, moving on instinct straight toward a point fixed deep in her consciousness.

Over the next two days Kim had kept a vigil for her at the Taech'ŏn railroad station. But neither he nor anyone else had seen her. Judging from her condition the day she left the clinic, Kim said, she probably wouldn't last long.

7

They threw rocks at me, they spit at my ugly carcass, they beat me up. But I didn't cry. No screams, no tears. I closed my eyes, I spread my arms and legs, I accepted it all like a sun-baked rice paddy soaking up water. And I felt the load lift from my shoulders. Each time they forced open my parched lips, the mouth I swore to the death I'd never open, and poured that burning liquid down my throat, I put my hands together and prayed: *Stop up the shameful breath of my life; split open my innards, swarming with maggots; fry my blood vessels, crooked as the veins in a dried-up branch; incinerate my groaning bones, enduring like shameful memories; burn my leathery skin. Let me disintegrate. Let me be dust.*

But always I would wake up, and there I would be, every last part of me. And somebody mocking or cursing me. So I willingly accepted my curse. At some point the air deep inside me started moving free. There was no stopping it and I opened my mouth wide to let it out. The people thought I was laughing and they bullied and beat me some more. I clamped my mouth dead shut. Because suddenly I was afraid of what might creep out: a foul-smelling liquid, dark green beetles, reptiles with shiny skins. The more tightly I shut my mouth, the worse some of those people attacked me. Somehow they knew I could talk. Would they have bullied me if I were a mute, like that man I met in the mountains? I let out that air because it was turning into a poison gas in my lungs. They must have thought I was laughing, especially if a sound leaked out with that air. What did they want to know? Why did they mistreat me when I didn't say anything?

Was it my name they wanted? My age? Or what? So many people looked at my mouth as if I had an awful secret, or was hiding something. I felt like asking them to rip out that curtain that covered my mind; then I could show them. But that was the least of their concerns. And is there really a black curtain covering my brain?

I was on a train. The train was going through a tunnel. It was a long tunnel, very long. At least I think it was a tunnel—I feel like there's a sponge inside my head that's sucking up all my memories. I was sitting in the jump seat between the coaches. It was dark outside. There was a face in the glass of the door at the end of the coach, a face I'd never seen before. It was flush against the other side, watching me. An old, worn-out face with no life to it. I got closer to the glass and from the other side the face got closer to me. It was the face of some mad bitch, a woman who'd slept too long, who'd kept her mouth shut too long. Her dirty face stuck to the glass like an insect that wouldn't go away.

The train was rushing toward something terrible, but I couldn't tell what. There was no one else with me between the coaches. The other passengers looked like they were sleeping. I thought I could hear, above the noise in the train, that woman in the glass panting.

I got up. She did too, as if she was reading my innermost thoughts. Her face was twisted with fear.

The train was going so fast a draft kept swishing in under the door. All I had to do was throw the door open, or else shake it a few times. So that the face of the woman sticking to the glass like an evil spirit would fall off and disappear into the night. . . .

All of a sudden that face reached out a hand for me, then faded in the distance. In its place was a small, lit-up train station with scarcely a person in sight. The train stopped and a few passengers got off. They glanced back at me as they headed toward the station. So many faces leave before I get to know them.

For an instant I thought that once and for all I had gotten rid of the ugly face that was watching me from the other side of the glass. But when the train rushed back into the night it reappeared, ghostlike. It was my sole companion on this long, distant journey, and I couldn't take my eyes off it—a face as ugly as the stink buried in my bowels, a murderous face among a den of goblins.

The monotonous rhythm of the wheels put me in a kind of trance, and I began slowly to get used to the face of my companion. I was afraid it would fall apart and melt into the night if I closed my eyes, so when the gray haze of sleep fell over me like a swarm of flies, I tried to fight it off.

Oh how I struggled to grab the black curtain that rustled ominously in the back of my head, waiting for a chance to attack! But I always missed. And every time I looked at that face it began to change. At one point the circles around the eyes disappeared, the discoloration and the shriveled wrinkles slowly faded, and color returned to the sunken cheeks. The face was completely transformed. It began to look familiar, a glowing face I saw somewhere between sleep and wakefulness. Why—it was my own face!

Many were the times I called up that face afterward. It was a face Mama could recognize. Brother too. The face I remember from before it all happened. The face I saw that morning before I went out with Mama, when I put on my fancy maroon dress, looked in the mirror, and said good-bye for the last time.

The train rode deeper into the night. No one passed through the space where I sat. The damp chill, the shadows frighteningly dark, the air hanging close and heavy about me—they reminded me of that night, whenever it was, that I had awakened all alone at the foot of a mountain. The thump of the wheels sounded like a military procession beneath the ground. Before I knew it I had closed my eyes. The thump grew louder and louder.

When next I looked, there in the window was a monster. The smiling face had darkened and shriveled, the hair had lost its flower, the ruddy cheeks were once more cavernous. The bony arms of that monster pawed at the air, the mouth opened wide, and I heard a sound like the gasp of a boiling kettle.

Something was about to happen. "Don't open your mouth!" I wanted to say. I looked at that face, wondering what to do, and a shudder swept through me. I just couldn't take my eyes away from it. My nose filled with the awful stink from that gaping mouth. I was afraid spiders and little stringy snakes would crawl out of it and bite my feet. I couldn't stand there any longer.

Suddenly a sound came from that mouth. At first it was soft, but then, as that underground thump grew steadily louder, it changed into a cry. That gaping mouth began to say things it shouldn't have: "I'm going to get rid of that black curtain for you. You said it's been covering your head—since when? Liar! Look at me now! Go ahead, attack me! I'm going to open up that skull of yours and pull out that curtain. You want me to tell you what happened? No? Come on, attack me! Look me in the eye, put those shameless lips to work, tell me all about that awful scene!"

The face started screaming. I pounded on the glass. I wanted to stop up that mouth before any more crazy, terrible words escaped from it. That twisted face, those struggling arms and legs, they attacked me.

"You say you can't see and yet you still feel the warmth of your mother's hand holding your hand tight! You say you're searching for your brother? You're trying to find his grave? Look at you! What do you think you're doing, carrying that bundle of squirming memories like they're a bunch of dirty insects! You've always been a damned idiot! A shade plant—that's what your teacher said! What are we going to do about you? Why don't you just disappear?"

I wanted to close that shouting mouth so badly, I banged on the glass with all my might. But I didn't have the strength. That face kept twitching, glaring, attacking me. . . . And then I felt a sweet sensation come over me: I should let the whole story spill out, let that face attack me, let it squeeze my throat and deliver me to a land of whiteness and peace. The temptation lasted but a moment, and then, as a face, another face, all the faces, appeared vaguely in the glass, I began shuddering from head to foot, overcome with shame.

I had to work faster, I had to shut up that mouth. My fists were useless, so I butted the window. Once, twice, three times, I lost count. Harder and harder. The glass broke with a sound of crystal clarity; the shouts faded; the face shattered and disappeared.

The train rushed deeper into the night. I still felt the draft beneath the door. People gathered around me, hands over their mouths in shock. Their faces flickered, barely visible. The conductor who had let me onto the train hurried over. His face was white. I got down on my knees and begged him silently. And then my tears gushed out. How long had it been since I'd cried like that?

It seemed like all the other passengers had awakened and were pressing toward me. My mind was growing hazy; I wanted to rouse myself, so I pinched my arms and legs. There was something I had to tell all those people before it was too late. Not that I wanted to explain why I'd killed that face in the window, or to ask forgiveness; I just wanted to talk. But something sticky was flowing into my eyes and it made their faces blurry. To talk to them, I had to get up. But I couldn't. The floor kept pulling me down like a magnet.

"She's trying to kill herself! Stop the train!"

Beneath my ear the underground procession continued. Yes, I was dying. The words I'd kept inside were insects gnawing at me. And all that was left of me was a shell. But I survived. Once again I survived. I was doomed to live.

The times I tried to recover the face that flashed in the glass! Not the twisted, convulsed face, but the plain yet wonderful face with the rosy cheeks and the flower in her hair. The face that Mama would recognize, and Brother too. That face had guided me all along, growing ever distant as it drifted over the horizon. Floating in the sky, smiling faintly, it had shown me the way out of that gray building where I was kept with other girls my age after the incident on the train.

How far have I come? How many nights have passed? No matter how far and how long I've run, it's right there behind me, that spring day. It feels just like yesterday. I take a quick glimpse back and there it is, right before my eyes.

That black curtain? It never existed. But for a long time I thought it did, because I wanted that curtain badly, wanted it to cover up everything. The memories of that day, clearer than water or glass, I painted over in white. Just like the horrible faces of those dead people were painted over. If I was going to be invisible, if I was going to die once and for all, white was the only color I could paint myself.

8

It was as if the girl had rediscovered herself. She began to scrub her face, her arms, her neck; she combed her tangled hair. But it was mostly a kind of playacting, and rarely did the tangles yield to the comb. She spent more and more time in front of the piece of mirror on the post near the drain. The hands grew busier with the comb, and the combing was accompanied by a constant, incomprehensible mutter punctuated by outcries. Her voice was so soft, her tongue worked so quickly, that the words couldn't be distinguished.

It became her morning ritual to rise quickly and fuss over her looks in front of the mirror, giggling with an exaggerated grin. It didn't seem, though, that her new interest in her appearance involved the clothes and shoes that the man had bought her. Sometimes she spent the day scrubbing the cement floor of his dwelling and arranging everything neatly.

Would her bruises and cuts never go away? The man had begun to feel as if one by one those hurts were penetrating his own body. Every instant he spent with the girl was painful, but he couldn't identify the source of that pain. His brutal, untamed heart throbbed and smoldered; he felt as if his skin were on fire.

Rumors began to swirl and surge in the cities, coursing swiftly from one lone mouth to the next like a taboo, rumors of a massacre in a city to the south, the details too horrible to be believed. Whenever a thread of these rumors reached the man's ears, he thought of the girl without understanding why. But then, after hearing talk of the nightmare in that city, he began to form an image of the city itself, an image that was framed, amplified, and detailed by the girl's unhealed wounds, her mindless laughter, the emptiness of her personality. The girl's present state had to be related to the events in that city, or else something comparable.

But of all the people she might choose to shadow, why *him*? And how had she found her way to his area? It was a monolithic enigma. He looked into his drink but found no answer.

She must have mistaken others as she had him, in each case responding to the call of some wavering image in her mind. Clearly she was incapable of asking herself who he was and why he observed her so anxiously.

A notion gradually took root in the man's mind: the girl had been sucked into the bloody swirl of that city to the south, then jettisoned near his home. The more he tried to deny this, the more he recalled the drawn, anguished faces that had communicated those rumors, faces more vivid than scenes revealed by a lightning flash in the dark of night. A few of those faces harbored a volatile, pulse-stopping anxiety—the faces of people who couldn't bring themselves to ask about the fate of their families in that city.

What about the girl, then? There she lay, fast asleep, her breathing strong and vigorous. But what if she died in her sleep? What if the next morning she didn't jerk awake as she usually did, what if he found her lying still in the corner like a pile of rags, what if the body he reached out and shook was cold and stiff? ... Horrified, the man found his camera, brought it close to her face, and snapped the shutter several times. Her only reaction to the flash was a feeble effort to turn over. And then she resumed her slow disintegration in the unfamiliar world of her profound slumber. That night the man couldn't sleep.

The girl's morning ritual continued unchanged. She opened the cloth bundle that was ever present beside her head as she slept, donned the maroon dress, clasped her hands behind her, and with an anxious smile observed her severed image in the fragment of mirror, now close, now from a distance. The man always found her hovering there when he returned from work. Come evening, she never failed to return the dress carefully to its cloth wrapper. The man replaced the fragment of mirror with a mirror large enough to show her from the waist up, but she didn't seem to notice the difference.

The man was relieved: now he knew how she spent her time. And eventually it made sense to him that the screws of her psyche should loosen one by one. How else could she have survived the mortal crush of her many nightmares?

It was much later that the man learned of her daytime absences. One day, on his way home, he saw her squatting in a sunny area of the marketplace, a withered flower in her tangled hair. Because he had never imagined her leaving his shed, he almost overlooked her. He was walking past her when she gave him the same vacuous smile she produced for the other passersby. The sight of him brought a faint glimmer to her eye, but not necessarily recognition. No one at the market took special notice of her—were they accustomed to seeing her there? Pathetically, a few coins, tossed out of charity, lay in the hem of her dress.

The market people said she'd been showing up late in the afternoon for the past week. The man told them she was a

relative, explained where he lived, and asked without convic-
tion that they contact him if anything should happen to her.
They would, they replied, equally unconvincingly. He took
the girl's hand. She rose light as dust and followed him obedi-
ently. The coins in the folds of her dress fell to the ground
with a lucid clink. The man's heart dropped. Perhaps in his
inarticulate way he feared that the girl would end up just like
those coins, slipping through his fingers, trampled by countless feet, covered with earth, and forgotten for all time.

Even more than this, what unsettled the man was his suspicion that her behavior, so inscrutable from without, was
part of a minutely detailed plan that was known only to her.
How else to explain the pattern of her life, which recurred
with such unchanging precision? If there was such a plan, it
was too dense for his mind to penetrate. Faced with this certainty, the man once again felt the presence of a mountainous
obstacle. He groaned, spat, then practically dragged the girl
home.

The man's life grew still more disordered. This was not
entirely the girl's fault. The fact was, she demanded nothing;
in no way did she interfere with him. She absorbed all and let
all be wrung out of her. But needless to say, she contributed to
the increasing irregularity of his life. The very sight of her
was like a nightmare. Her utter lack of response pained him.
What could he do to awaken her? He hadn't a clue. If he
couldn't return her to normalcy, wasn't there at least a way he
could transform her into something resembling a human
being? It was maddening. Yes, the man would tell us, he was
going crazy. And if he ended up losing his mind like that girl,
then so be it.

The man took a day off from work. While the girl was finishing her morning ritual, he left the shed and waited tediously
in the alley for her to emerge. Finally, there she was in her

maroon dress. She was wearing the enameled shoes he had bought her, but they were on the wrong feet. Her lips were serrated with scarlet smudges of lipstick. She turned halfway back, but without so much as a glance at the man as he smoked a cigarette, then continued on like a sleepwalker, hands groping the air. She passed the market and continued haltingly toward the main street, ignoring those she bumped into along the way. Occasionally she paused to pass a hand over her hair or smooth a pleat in her dress. Without breaking stride, brisk-walking passersby turned back toward the girl with peculiar smiles.

At the main street the girl promptly turned left, and at the end of that street, in one smooth motion, she turned left again. This became the riverside road.

The man, ten yards behind, followed her toward the steps to the riverside construction site. It was down those steps that she had followed him two months earlier. And there he froze, seized by an instinctive fear that had lain dormant since then. He looked all around. It occurred to him to snatch the girl and lock her up at home, but curiosity got the better of him and he continued to follow her.

He saw her, before she reached the bottom of the steps, creep into the woods that separated the river and the road above. He hastened down to where she had left the steps, and there he watched her. A short distance into the open woods she found a confined space among the trees. She lay down and stretched out, shielding her face from the sun. He wondered if she was singing in that halting way of hers, as she had the day he first saw her. He recalled with a shudder the tune she had hummed so monotonously then. In his mind it sounded unrealistically clear.

He squatted on the steps, let his heavy head droop, and waited. Waited for her to sing or hum as she had that day.

Barring that, he hoped she would fall asleep there until evening. He felt no impatience; the familiar scenes of the riverside seemed to calm his unsettled mind. Neither bored nor preoccupied, he continued to wait.

He looked up, thinking he had heard a large bird flapping overhead. It was the girl, crawling up the slope as smartly as an animal, light and quick on her feet. By the time he had retraced his steps back up the hill she was out of the woods and headed for a crosswalk. *To look at her now, you wouldn't think she was loony.*

She came to a halt in front of the red crossing signal, brushed the straw and twigs from her hair, and gently smoothed the seat of her dress. Across the road was a graveyard. To the man it resembled a huge forest of tombstones sprouting from an endless series of bumpy terraces. The signal turned green, and the girl hurried across the road. The man followed. Something told him she wouldn't look back even if he caught up with her and dogged her steps the way she had his that day.

Her route described the crooked line of someone lost in thought. The man wanted to run up to her, get her attention, talk to her. But he was afraid of her empty gaze, certain that along with the reflection of himself to be found in her pupils he would also find rejection.

The girl walked more quickly. Countless paths partitioned the burial mounds; without the slightest hesitation she chose one of them.

The man saw her, at the end of that path, scamper to the upper tiers of gravestones. He stopped along a narrow path that was out in the open and exposed to the sun and looked for a place to hide. *That sun.* . . . Its rays were a scourge that suddenly made him feel naked. He reversed his direction.

Utter silence. A standstill, a dead end—a trap? The girl didn't seem to have an objective among the endless array of gravestones. Instead, with ceremonial precision she collected sprigs from the occasional bouquets, and in front of this naked stone and that she would squat and place a flower. And at one such stone she slowly began to sway. The man imagined her lips beginning to move. Her swaying gradually intensified in time with the movements of her mouth. The man heard nothing, but knew that even if he did, he wouldn't understand. What she was mouthing was like floating dust particles. The girl jerked from side to side and her voice, suddenly audible, grew to a scream that tore at the man's ears, and then a shriek that shattered the oppressive silence of the graveyard, the war cry of a wayward spirit enclosed in a massive wall, a blast that set the gravestones trembling. The man fell on his side, closed his eyes, and listened, waiting for the crack that would form in the wall and the flood of sound that would pour through it.

But then it was over. Silence returned. The man saw the girl rise unsteadily, turn, and walk away. Her face bore a tranquility he had never seen before. She had placed a few withered flowers in her hair.

The girl's brisk pace took her quickly to the main street. There she ignored every face, every scene, smiling ambiguously at the visage that occupied her mind, moving mechanically at some absurd task the man couldn't identify.

And then, sure enough, she arrived at the marketplace and hunkered down where the man had earlier discovered her. After sprucing herself up, she gazed dully at the passersby, flinching at the feet that filed past directly in front of her, now giggling, now somberly caressing the backs of her bony hands.

The man walked past her like everyone else and returned home. He waited. And before sunset she returned. Ignoring his presence, she went straight to her spot, lay down, and seemed to fall asleep at once.

The next day, and the day after, were repeats of the previous one except that the amount of time she spent in the woods or at the market varied slightly. After four days of this routine the man gave up following her. In the morning the girl would toss and turn in her sleep, and the withered flowers ended up strewn beside her head like so many dead moths.

Those four days were a period of despair for the man, a feverish, inconsolable despair to which the minor collapses, the occasional irritations of everyday life, offered no comparison. For in following the girl he had finally come face to face with the world she inhabited—the netherworld occupied by the insane. The man felt himself slipping slowly into that subterranean place. To him it was a world of white, the white ash of cremated corpses. A place where suffering was consumed like flesh.

One day she would slide down that white cavity, and all too quickly, before she could produce her characteristic giggle, she would find herself sucked cheerfully into the happiness of utter oblivion, to disappear forever into a confinement that marked the beginning of a living death. By the time the man realized how fast she was riding toward that cavity, it was too late. He was powerless to stop her, incapable of solving the massive enigma that loomed over her as always. Suddenly he recalled an amazing fact: in all the weeks she had lived with him, the girl hadn't once volunteered a word. His heart burned. Confronted with her vacant gaze, he felt betrayed.

What more could he do for her? Only this: he produced the three photos he had taken while she was asleep. Someone, somehow, would recognize her, even though her eyes were closed. For the first time in his life the man tried to mentally construct a "found" notice for the newspaper, phrasing it one way and then another: *Family or acquaintances of the above are kindly requested to contact. . . . Name: unknown. Age: early teens. Height: approximately 4'7". Distinguishing characteristics*—. Here the man was stymied. He observed her face with its wrinkles and pulpy discolorations, her cadaverous cheeks, her dull gaze, and he wondered how much of this damage had occurred before her descent into that netherworld. He decided to skip over the distinguishing characteristics. For he was convinced she would be recognized no matter how many transformations she had undergone. Selecting the photo that showed most of the girl's face, he hurried outside.

9

Yes, it's true, that black curtain never existed. It's something my devil hands wove. They wove it nice and thick and then they hung it up. And I told myself, "Girl, don't you ever think back." Because if I did, then the fabric of that curtain would wear. And when the curtain finally wore through, the events of that day would come back to life as if a searchlight had hit them. But there were days, many days, when I thought I would starve, and on those days I wanted so badly to forget my hunger and to keep myself awake that I forgot my promise. Not that I tried to forget what had happened. It was just that a train of memories came back to me. I couldn't help it. And now that black curtain that I wove with my own hands is all worn out. A curtain that never really existed.

Those men in suits told us Brother was dead. I've always thought that's when Mama started acting strange. But maybe not. Sometimes I wonder if those men really came to our

house. Or maybe it was after Mama learned about Brother
that they brought the white envelope. I don't know, it's all
mixed up. I feel like I've been stuck in a bag along with everything that's happened, past and present, and the bag's being
shaken all up.

I still don't know what Mama was doing downtown. I
think there was more to it than just going to the market. In
the evening she'd come home with some papers and ask me
to read them to her. She couldn't read very well herself. But I
was afraid I'd make a mistake and so of course I didn't want
to do it. Then Mama would start screaming and pounding
on her head, and finally I would stutter my way through the
papers. I had no idea what the words meant—"petition,"
"supplicant," and all the rest—I just read them. It wasn't
much fun.

"Don't worry, we're not going to starve," she said. And
with that she stopped going out at dawn to stock her market
stall. She was always going around seeing people. She came
home so tired I couldn't bear to look at her.

One day I got home from school and heard Mama screaming and wailing inside. I thought she was having a fight with
someone. I worked up my courage and went in, but no one
was there except Mama. She was rolling around on the floor,
grabbing the hem of her blouse like she was going to rip it
apart. I figured it had something to do with her work at the
market. Because there in front of her was a ripped-up notice
in a yellow envelope, the kind she received when there was a
problem in connection with her business.

After that Mama was sick in bed for over a week. But nobody came visiting, unless you count that mutt of Sun-dŏk's,
who came around looking for something to eat. I skipped
school two days and just stretched out next to Mama. That
was fun. Mama didn't budge, she felt so bad, so I was able to

lie around the whole day long, except for when she wanted some more water or another quilt.

After Mama went back to the market, her heart seemed to be in her work again. She said she needed to make more money. It's all so hazy now, but I remember that she left at dawn and she wouldn't get home till after I was asleep. When the glare from the naked light bulb woke me, I would see her licking her thumb to count the money she had earned that day. That sight comforted me and in no time I was asleep again.

The long winter vacation passed without Brother, and then that day arrived, in the month of May, at the height of spring.

If it wasn't for that day, everything could have worked out differently. Mama could have lived, instead of dropping to the ground with holes in her! I wish these hands of mine would rot—I wish I could stick them in acid that would eat them away! I can still feel the touch of Mama's hand—her burning, feverish hand. It makes me shudder. It's too late to change anything. No matter how I try to put those thoughts out of my mind, that sensation is there to awaken me, to make me get up. I can't avoid it. How can I put an end to the storm inside my head? Heaven will punish me. To avoid an even worse punishment, I have to go to Brother and tell him all that's happened. He's there in his grave, a dark hole where the chill of night creeps up his back. He can't wait till I arrive. Will he recognize me now that I look so frightful? If I could get back the face he would recognize, if I could get it back just for a moment, maybe he would remember me, remember me in spite of the monster's words spewing from my mouth. Maybe he would forgive me.

Brother, here I am. I rested on the way because I had to walk so far. You recognize me, don't you? Say it: "Of course I do. Yes, it's you." Say it! I've got so many things to tell you. I'll put this flower in my hair—there, you can recognize me now, right? And I bet you remember this dress. It's the one Mama took me downtown to buy so I could wear it when you came home for the Harvest Moon Festival. You said it was pretty, remember? And you said you'd get me prettier ones, lots of them, and I'd make someone a fine wife. But you don't have to buy those dresses now. As long as you recognize me, nothing else matters. Gee, I've got so many things to talk about. I can't figure out why I was so scared till now. Just make sure you don't put your hands over your ears while I'm talking. If you do, I'll turn to dust. Now that I think about it, I've died and come back to life again and again. I'm sick of it. Thousands of times I wished I could just turn into dust and float off silently into the infinity of the universe.

Okay, now I'm going to tell you what happened that day. I'm not exactly sure which day it was, but I do know that for several days before, all the neighbors had been standing around in small groups whispering about something. The streets were quiet, and they looked longer and wider than usual because all the children were being kept inside. The grown-ups gathered on the streets. They were frowning, and every now and then they looked up at the sky and heaved a sigh; I think something was eating away at them inside. The weather was fine; everywhere there was the sweet scent of a flower I didn't know. But there was something else in the air, something sharp and painful.

I was getting bored without anyone to play with, and Mama was getting more and more wrapped up in something I didn't understand. She acted like she was putting her heart into her work at the market, struggling for the sake of a few coins, but I knew it was just a cover for that other business she was caught up in.

I think it might have rained that morning. But I don't remember getting rained on—isn't it strange? In my mind I
have an image of a day that was so bone dry I thought the roof
was going to burst into flames. I can't put it into words, but I
felt I could understand why the grown-ups in our neighborhood looked worried when they saw the young people leaving.

Well, I wonder if it really rained that morning, or if I just
thought it rained because of Mama crying all the previous
night. Anyway, I woke up to a gray dawn and there was
Mama sitting in front of the mirror, patting down her hair.
She was all dressed up in her old-fashioned skirt and jacket,
that light pink linen outfit. She reminded me of a newly-
wed. Her face in the mirror jiggled for a moment, and
though it was still kind of dark I could see a sparkle in her
eyes. When she noticed me watching her, she told me not to
go to school that day.

The strange thing was, she said it so tenderly, not in the
high-and-mighty tone she usually used with me. I jumped
out of bed and said I'd go with her to the market. "No, girl,
I'm not going to the market. I've got someplace else to go, and
don't you even think about tagging along! Oh, what am I
going to do with you?" But I was already fetching water to
wash my face. "What's the idea, running around like this first
thing in the morning? You want to die before your time?"
Now she was getting choked up.

Suddenly she turned and looked straight at me. There was
something odd about her look. Something that reminded me
of the shaman man. His eyes used to light up before he did his
dance on the blades of the fodder choppers, when he was
looking over the people gathered around and picking out the
ones who weren't pure. He never asked any of those people to
leave, but that look of his was enough to frighten them off.

Mama's expression scared me in that way, but I couldn't look away from her. I knew Mama wasn't going to the market that morning; I felt she was going to leave me forever. Everything came into focus at that instant. I was going to latch onto her and not let go. I must have looked pale and breathless as I stared at her, trying to plant myself in her gaze. But by then she wasn't focusing on me anymore. Like a woman possessed, she clutched her purse and opened the door, without a look back. My heart dropped. I started moving in a hurry. My body was moving much faster than my mind. I *had* to follow Mama, and from that point things happened with dizzying speed. I changed into my fancy maroon dress. I surprised myself when I looked in the mirror. My face looked unfamiliar, like it was lit up with a blue flame. Something told me I should say good-bye to that face. I even swept back my hair and produced a smile. Once again I bid my face good-bye.

I ran after Mama. Already she was far down the alley, but I didn't need to lose my head and call out to her. To go downtown she had to take a bus, and I knew I could catch up to her at the bus stop. I took one last look at our house. I had a hunch that Mama and I wouldn't be returning.

That early in the morning, the streets were practically deserted. But even in the dim light of dawn I could make out at least half a dozen people in the distance at the bus stop. I can't remember if Uncle Pak was at his little shop. It wasn't too early for him to be there. Maybe he didn't open it that day— or maybe I was too involved with Mama to notice. I was terrified that she would sink into the ground or dissolve into the dawn mist. I heard a menacing voice inside my head: *If you lose her now, you'll never find her again.* Yes, I'd been losing Mama little by little. What if she left me once and for all? . . .

I tried not to run. I *couldn't* run. It was as if Mama and I had an unwritten rule against it. But I walked as fast as I could. It's a wonder I didn't fall on my face.

I hated my short legs. Why wouldn't my heart slow down? I wished my muscles would obey me. Finally I caught up with Mama, grabbed her skirt tie with both hands, and buried my face in her chest. I was out of breath.

I wish I had dropped dead then and there. Mama immediately began spanking me. "You little devil! Why can't you stay home? You want to get killed? Get going—now!" she screamed. I let her hit me, and then she gave me a shove toward home. I fell down in the street. "Don't you come back here, or else!" I jumped up, ran after her, and caught her by the waist of her skirt. "For once in your life will you listen to your mother? You little fool—go back home and stay there!" She was losing her voice. "I am *not* going to run off and leave you. I'll be back tonight."

But I didn't believe her and I grabbed onto her all the more. Fear swept over me. I bawled, I stamped my feet, I hooked my hands inside her waistband with all my might and wouldn't let her budge. I begged her. The funny thing was, it seemed like all those other people looked away. And, you know, I can't remember a single one of their faces.

The bus arrived. Mama made one last attempt to cut me loose, but I kept hold of the hem of her skirt and climbed on behind her.

Maybe I fell asleep next to Mama, because I have no idea where we went on that bus. I do remember holding her around the waist. And once, for a moment, Mama took my two hands in hers. And squeezed them, I think. She was looking outside. From the side her face looked twisted and ugly.

They wouldn't let our bus go downtown. We had to get off on a deserted road on the outskirts of the city and walk. Oh, how we walked! Actually the distance to downtown was nothing compared with how far I walked afterward, but at the time, it felt like we just weren't getting any closer.

It was all because of that bitter, stinging smell. It penetrated your nose even if you held your breath; it made the road seem longer than those roads you walk in a nightmare, the ones that never come to an end. I let go of Mama's skirt, squatted, and threw up the yucky fluid in my empty stomach. And then fear grabbed hold of me. Mama was far out ahead. I ran and stumbled after her.

The moment that smell hit me, everything changed—trees, mountains, sky, roofs. It put my insides in turmoil, it penetrated my brain and stuck there. For an instant I regretted having followed Mama. But then I realized it was much too late for regrets.

We went up and down dozens of alleys I'd never seen before, moving incredibly fast. I saw Mama as a soaring dancer, a crane flying toward a great flock of other cranes that choked the alleys. It was a day for which no picture, no tapestry of words existed.

For a time Mama stood by herself, apart from the crowd, her arms wrapped around herself. She looked at me as I held tight to her, trembling. And then there were helicopters circling in the sky. People started to shout all together. They sounded like a flock of cranes spreading their wings and beating the air. Mama shoved me inside the dark entrance to a building and shut the door. As fast as I could I ran back outside. Without a word she scooped me up and threw me back inside. I got up and ran out again. No words were exchanged between us, only harsh breathing. Mama's face was ugly and frightening. I think she was looking that way on purpose to show me how disgusted she was. This silent pestering contest, repeated numerous times, left us both exhausted.

Finally I grabbed Mama's wrist with both hands and wouldn't let go. Again Mama danced like a mad crane. There was a flood of faces and outcries, and always the bitter smell, and we rode that current until finally I was part of it. The tide rose, spilled onto a wide street, a current of noise and waves of people that carried me forward, always forward. Mama's hand was like a vise. The tide of people surged onward, ever onward, pulling me away from her till I thought my crotch would split. The cries filled my ears, as if they had descended from the heavens; I imagined the current rising to the level of my mouth, and I couldn't breathe. Over and over, the ebb and flow. I couldn't bear to look at Mama's face anymore. She was in another world, a world where people were dancing. Her face had a reddish gleam that blinded me. But still she wanted a connection with the world where I remained, and she held fast to my hand. Behind me was a chorus of faces, unforgettable faces.

Suddenly there was a tremendous outcry. Something had happened up ahead. The massive current began to come apart. Gleaming faces became twisted, torn, flipped back, were thrown to the pavement in a heap. They were dyed with blood, bright red blood.

All at once the wide street emptied. People ran in all directions, screaming, moaning, throwing up blood, falling forward. I saw glinting blades of steel, clubs flailing madly. Faces with cruel grins chased the fleeing flocks. Crushed faces, twisted faces, faces. . . . Faces that had lost their glow, faces that had grown expressionless in an instant. I had to get away.

And then I heard it, a sound like someone walking alone in the dead of night. It became the sound of someone running after us. And then it was more than one, and they were getting closer. I shut my eyes and didn't turn back. Someone caught Mama from behind, and faster than a sound something ripped into her chest. My mother's chest.

It happened so quickly. *That's why you have to open your eyes wide and look! Look at that one instant!* When Mama's face was thrown back, when she turned to face me, Mama with holes in her, her mouth open, only the whites of her eyes showing. And I. . . . *That's it, call it all up, take your time, every last detail, until your bones dissolve in grief.*

Her neck was bent back like a bow, as if she were performing a strenuous dance. Her face turned toward me; her mouth was slightly open, but no sound came from it.

Now I want you to listen very carefully, because I'm going to tell you what you did at that instant. Every last detail.

You couldn't remove your eyes from the dark liquid flowing from the hole in Mama's tummy. Suddenly a chorus of outcries flooded your ears; you heard each part of that chorus clearly. Just as suddenly Mama's hand felt hard as a rock, but it held yours more tightly, it radiated warmth, it felt as if it would burn your hand up. And because of the pain she felt, pain she could not transform into a cry, you jerked your hand back and forth insanely, trying to free it from hers.

You closed your eyes to avoid the sight of Mama's twisted face. Or maybe you were looking at the hideous sight of the whites of her eyes. But in this human whirlpool you couldn't free yourself from Mama's hardened grip. As you were pulled by the bulk of your collapsing mother, one by one you cruelly freed yourself from her clawlike fingers.

And what then? Focus your eyes and play back those events that happened within the space of a minute. Play them back even if they poison you, even if your blood should dry up in the long-suppressed heat of your breath.

And finally—you stepped on Mama's tightly flexed arm and freed your hand. Her skin and muscles felt slippery. You stepped on them as hard as you could. And then you ran away from the moving masses of people. You ran, perhaps stepping on faces, perhaps kicking them aside; you ran down alleys, not looking back, your eyes closed, not knowing where you were going. You ran, you fell, you got up and ran, till you could no longer hear the chaos of footsteps behind you. You were afraid Mama's hands would reach out over you from behind, and you placed your own hands in your armpits for protection. The slipperiness of Mama's arm beneath your foot, the warmth of her hand in yours—you shook your head over and over to get rid of the image of your mother flickering so clearly before your eyes. The battle cry still followed you, you couldn't shake the sound of the footsteps behind you; you closed your eyes; you were so out of breath you thought you would vomit blood.

I can never return to that day. To the place where I committed that terrible crime. Where I stamped on Mama's hand, her arm, her empty gaze, so that I alone could live.

The whites of Mama's eyes were looking at me. She was looking at me without blame, her breath stilled, a motionless mass of bones and flesh. She's probably been transported to a place where she can't feel the rough shovel blade even if it cuts her, a place where her wounds are painless and no longer bleed. What did she want to tell me when her lips opened that last time, when she turned her twisted face toward mine, a face that somehow looked peaceful?

Mother had a dream, and I, her daughter, had crushed it.

I can never go back to our home. All those people would remember me. They would remember the hellishly long time I spent struggling to free my hand from Mama's. That awful news must have spread like wildfire from mouth to mouth among all those people. There would always be nagging rumors, shocking rumors. They're waiting for me back there, waiting for me armed with sticks and timbers, night or day, lanterns lit.

And now I have nowhere to go. Nowhere except Brother's grave. I have to tell him, even if it kills him again. Then I can turn into dust and disappear into the ground. I'm not afraid anymore. I'll rip off that black curtain and my ugly face will rise like the moon over his grave. Tomorrow my moldy body will be drying in the sun for everyone to see.

I have to tell Brother everything. Before all of my other brothers rise from their graves and get into some other trouble.

10

Does any of us remember how long we stayed in Taech'ŏn? How long we lingered in the gloom of the impossibility of finding her? We realized that with each passing day we increased the distance and the time between her and us, but we felt lethargic, almost paralyzed, as if we were waiting for everything to go irrevocably wrong. We were beyond fretfulness.

It was evident that she hadn't left Taech'ŏn by train. We didn't study the map anymore. We didn't approach people on the street, didn't show them that old photo, no longer asked useless questions. Kim's degeneration—a monster he nurtured to lessen the hurt of a past gone wrong—harmonized with our lethargy. We stayed in the lodgings he offered us, sleep and alcohol eroding our raw youthfulness.

Occasionally we reminded ourselves that she had not taken a train out of Taech'ŏn. But so much time had passed that this piece of evidence ceased to be remarkable; we were like a container of liquid that shifts when moved, only to resume its original position. When Kim got drunk he would insist that the girl was dead and gone, somewhere off in the countryside. We could continue to wait, he said, but at some point we might as well visit the police stations in the Taech'ŏn area to see if an accidental death had been reported.

But we clung to an irrational hope, a hope that one day she would miraculously appear before our eyes. When for brief moments we thought clearly about the situation, we flailed ourselves with the realization that weariness had made us superstitious.

Eventually we resumed our search. We had found to our surprise that in this region there were several people just like the girl who, if not necessarily for the same reason, were wandering around in the grip of some compulsion. But we could find no one who had seen her—only girls who fit her description. We found ourselves unable to return to the lives we had led, unless we located her. But even if we had found her, could we really have returned to those lives as if nothing had happened?

Her soul was out there, roaming about, stirring up the dark of night like a will-o'-the-wisp. . . . And then there was our friend—how could we fill the void he had left? How could we restore the space originally provided for him in the family register, a space prematurely shortened and blocked off, a chipped tooth in a comb? To the dead, death is not an event. It happens, harsh and vivid, only to the living. For death has no answers; it leaves incomplete that which should be completed.

If we were to believe Kim—the only one known to us to have seen her recently at close range—it would surely be more painful for us to see her alive than dead. Because her life had been turned upside down in a single instant; because she had been trapped in a chamber of insanity, a chamber darker than death, which offered no possibility of bringing her life to completion. What torture for us the living to see a person in a state of walking death! People often describe such a person as utterly mad. It sounds so simple. Just call someone mad and there, the world is back in order again. You gather with others, bring up familiar names, slap your knee and say you've just heard that poor so-and-so has lost her mind, and put on a sad face. Maybe it was better, as Kim had said, if the girl was dead and gone; maybe it was better if she didn't reappear before us.

Finally, while Kim was briefly away from home, we left him our address and departed. We felt like thieves, or like a confidence man abandoning a desperate lover while she sleeps. We had left our friend's (and her) hometown more than a month earlier, and by the time we left Taech'ŏn we felt that this period was unacceptably long. We caught the night train. Abandoning our plan of inquiring at every train station along the way, ignoring what lay outside the windows, we ruthlessly canvassed our despondent imaginations for help and we listened intently to the sound of the wheels on the rails, for we knew intuitively that the girl had taken this same journey long before we had ever boarded the train.

Later that night we were awakened by one of our group. He was visibly startled. Instinctively our gazes shot outside. We were approaching Ch'ŏnan. The one who had awakened us didn't say a word. Instead, slack-jawed, he pointed toward the far end of the coach. In the very last seat we saw the sleeping face of a girl in her early teens. She was slumped over, her wildly tangled hair half covering her face. It was a grimy face, with hollow cheeks and sunken eyes. But her profile was one of indescribable peace: a smile rested lightly on her face as she lay there swathed in sleep. Resting on the frayed knees of her cotton pants was a small cloth bundle that was so dirty you couldn't make out the pattern. Her twiglike arms were absolutely still, but an occasional tremor rose on her smiling lips.

When we had fully awakened, we, along with our friend, came to the sinking realization that our eyes had deceived us. We took a deep breath, and there at the end of the coach we discovered, soundly asleep, not a girl but a country woman in her mid-twenties about whom there was absolutely nothing out of the ordinary.

This illusion lingered long in our minds. That supreme bliss we thought we had seen kept resurfacing in our memory, wiping out all previous images of the girl. That smile seemed to be mocking the haste with which we, her brother's class-mates, had set out in search of her, and now that we were wide awake we spent the hours remaining till dawn wonder-ing exactly why we had launched this search. To comfort our lost friend with the knowledge that we had found her? To pacify the soul of their departed mother? To fulfill our sense of obligation to do something after what had happened that day in that city to the south? Or because we couldn't live with ourselves if we did nothing? Did we want a quick cure for the suffering that we in our immaturity felt? Were we motivated by a masochistic desire to find in that girl a corporeal vestige of that horrible day? In wanting to protect a girl who was al-ready wasted psychologically, were we merely indulging in a cheap excuse for humanitarianism? Did we, like that wan-dering girl, wish to keep awake for fear of sleep? Or were we trying simply to live on in spite of the cancerous nightmares we carried inside us?

It was much later that we understood the meaning of the smile we had glimpsed on that phantasm. And we waited for the day when, ever so naturally, she would appear to us wearing that smile.

Dawn approached from beyond the window.

The first anniversary of the death of our friend drew near. Autumn was passing, and we still hadn't located his sister. We all gathered at our boardinghouse for the ceremony.

Suddenly the door to the room was flung open, and there stood the friend who had awakened us on the train and ushered us into that otherworldly illusion. In his hand was a creased page from a newspaper. He spread it out and indicated a photo of a face at the bottom. The image was faint, but we could make out the closed eyes and the vacuous smile playing about the lips. It clearly resembled the face in the photo of our friend's sister that we'd obtained from their neighbors. *Family or acquaintances of the above are kindly requested to contact. . . . Name: unknown. Age: early teens. Height: approximately 4′7″.* We checked the date of the newspaper. Already more than a month and a half ago. We sprang up at once, uncertain though we felt about finding her.

We located the address given in the notice, a shedlike basement dwelling. We knocked on the glass pane of the door and presently a tall, imposing man with a pale face appeared. He looked to be half a dozen years older than we. Somehow we were jolted by the sight of him, but in no time this feeling was replaced by a peculiar sense of intimacy. His name was Chang, he told us, and he worked at a construction site down by the river. We noticed he had a slight stutter. When we mentioned the purpose of our visit, he grew distracted. Stuttering even more, he began to talk about her. It soon became clear that she wasn't there.

Haltingly he explained how she had followed him home seemingly at random. As we listened we came to understand the source of the intimacy we felt with him, and the reason the girl had followed him among all the people she must have encountered along the river. Something in his profile and his build suggested the friend we had lost a year earlier.

The man spoke for a few hours. We managed not to interrupt, and as we listened to his monologue punctuated with sobs, we felt as if we were dropping into a bottomless gulf. He constantly reproached himself. He begged us to find her, or to tell him how to find her. But we had nothing to offer him, not even an empty promise.

Afterward, leaving our address as we always did, we returned to our boardinghouse. And there we gathered to write the letter that would occupy the humble ceremonial table we would use for the ritual a few days hence.

We sat in silence, and for the briefest instant we imagined a girl we had never seen, a smile that seemed to hover about us, a withered flower in her hair, and her maroon dress swaying as she dropped lightly to a sitting position in front of a grave that didn't contain her brother.

Whisper Yet

Whisper Yet

If that's what you really want, my child. If you want to be an assassin, the assassin in your comics, then yes. I can see you walking soundlessly through streams of mysterious moonlight, scaling walls impossibly high; I can hear your nimble, light-footed steps as you pass by the village of the unforgivable. If you were an assassin, what would your weapon be? I can see you in the middle of a vast plain under the moon's white halo, trying to decide which way your path lies. But I can't visualize the weapon rising from your hand. Perhaps a small wand emitting night light? Like the light of your eyes, so clear and bright that they glow green in the night? Yes. Your weapon must not have a sharp cutting edge. Like light or air, it must be impalpable, yet it must make everyone stand stock-still before it and look about himself. Yes, my child. If it is so, you may become the child assassin of your comics. If in that way you can stand in the face of a tidal wave. If in that way you can transcend the hearts and minds of those who are hurting.

Allow me a cigarette, my child. A wisp of smoke disinfects the inside of the belly. Like the fog. Like the light of the setting sun.

Look at the woods out there. Ah, why should I long for the bramble patch that once seemed so desolate? It's no use. Whoever has lingered at dusk on the shore of a woodland lake knows. Knows that the boundary between day and evening, water and sky, one utterance and another becomes blurred at a certain moment. Knows precisely where that boundary becomes blurred. Isn't the world's most beautiful scenery located at such boundaries? Tears flow from my eyes at such a moment. Why? Is it because of you? I see now that no tear is ever entirely pure. For dissolved in joy there is sorrow, just as the most extreme sorrow invariably brings with it, however small, an expectation of happiness. So tears are like a narcotic: if not allowed to flow at their appointed time, they awaken the convulsions that lurk in the depths of our very existence. So, my child, we must learn to see the tears of those who cry unseen, or who want to cry but cannot.

Yes, it would be a good thing. If only people were honest enough to cry when they must, my child, flowers would bloom inside my belly. Why there? Because nothing is more honest than the inside of the belly. Doesn't everything happen because of what happens inside the belly? After the world was made and since the very first day humans appeared in it, has it ever been different? Long live the inside of the belly! Inside the belly where once you were. Yes, long may it live! I must put on my sunglasses. The sun is still hot.

An orchard in northern Kyŏnggi Province. We were spending a week there, a week our daughter had so wished for—a *vacance*, as we called it. When she was little our daughter often confused *vacance* with Pakk'asŭ, a popular tonic, giving us many a laugh. There she sat now, wearing sunglasses with pink frames, the plastic lenses nearly black, her lips thrust out in a pout, arms folded like a grown-up's. Though I could not see her expression, I had the impression she resented the blazing sun and its heat, and the blandness of the scenery. Seen through my heavily tinted sunglasses, the sea, the yacht, and the goldfish in her diary were a jumble, the sea bluer, the yacht whiter, and the three goldfish more orange and undulating, as if in violent revolt.

"My child, you look just like Greta Garbo the way you sit."

"Who's Greta Garbo?" she answered sullenly, staring into the still scenery where the light of the white-hot sun cast the shadows of the trees in clear relief. She looked like she might burst into a tantrum.

"The most beautiful woman in the world—at least that's what Mama thinks."

"Yeah?" she said, flashing a smile. I returned to my afternoon doze, and my child to her summer vacation picture diary.

A lake. Is that the right word for such a small water hole? Still, that's what everyone called it. This lake peeked shyly from a thicket of scrub at the foot of a hill and a soft, clear light seemed always to play about its shores. Located in such an out-of-the-way place, it was a welcome sight to a person clambering down the hillside at dusk. Water striders making innumerable tiny dimples on the surface—in my mind I can still see very clearly the barely visible legs of those insects and the busy flapping of the birds. Small and nondescript though they were, those birds flew no less impressively than the hawks soaring confidently among the mountain summits. They traced large circles low in the sky, then dropped down to skim the narrow surface of the water before soaring up and around in more low circles, ultimately to catch and consume small fish. They might have been kingfishers. Evening meals in flight. Yes, birds in the wild are sometimes more elegant than people.

The monsoons had been awful that summer. One day, after they had finally passed, we saw that a lake had formed. And with the lake came the birds, and with the birds the water striders. . . . Anybody who has spent hours sitting by that lake knows: from whichever side you looked, you saw only half the sky reflected on the surface of the water. For a very long time I was unhappy that the sky was not reflected in its entirety. When I close my eyes, the first thing I see is the lake reflecting all of the sky, except where it's in the shade of the trees. For a long time I thought the lakeshore would be the place to welcome you into the world. Why? It was probably the lonesomeness evoked by the scenery there. On the very day you first opened your eyes I wanted you to see the lonesomeness of the deserted orchard. Not the closed room with the pink curtains and the extra-tiny bed and the humidified air, but the field spreading beyond the lake and its desertlike thicket of scrub. I wanted you to see the starting point of your life. Those who have seen the wasteland come to feel a deep sense of shame about life. And they do not expect too much from it.

"My, this lake is lonesome."

"What lake? The lake where Dad went fishing?"

"No."

"Mama, you're talking to yourself again!"

One of my husband's friends had sold his business and re-settled his family at this countryside orchard. If not for his suggestion, my family and I would have spent this summer, like other summers, watching Hong Kong martial arts films or heaven knows what other videos, with scarcely a glimpse of the outdoors. Neither of us relished the prospect of fight-ing our way through the hordes of people packing the popu-lar vacation spots—assuming we could afford to go to those spots in the first place. Nor were we as a couple resourceful enough to devise a new and different form of vacation. So when my husband's friend suggested we look after the or-chard during their absence—he was taking his family, in-cluding his parents, to Guam or Saipan or some such vacation spot where the coconut palms sway like they do in calendar photos—we for our part, and each for a different reason, welcomed it with shouts of joy. Finally we were going on a vacation! My husband gave me a conspiratorial wink, probably thinking about the fishing hole that was supposed to be thirty minutes away, while our daughter could hardly sleep thinking about the *vacance* she had so wished for as well as our promise to let her feed the chickens and ducks at the orchard. As for me . . . the single word "orchard" aroused a strange madness in the depths of my mind, and gazing into the distance, I nodded.

But this orchard was different from the one I had conjured up in my reveries. It was too large and luxuriant, not a single water hole anywhere but noisy animals everywhere. With thirty-some chickens, a dozen ducks, and a turkey, peacock, and parrot to boot, and with more high-priced garden plants and shrubs than fruit trees, it was more a zoo and a nursery than an orchard. In the morning, following the instructions of my husband's friend, we turned on all the whirling irrigators and watered by hand those spots the hoses didn't reach, and by the time we finished feeding all the birds—having had no chance to rest—our morning was gone. Even feeding the birds was no easy task; our daughter quickly followed me at a distance with an unhappy expression as I made the rounds of the smelly bird cages with a feeder. It was heavy labor.

Still, I was happy. An orchard. The orchard I had known was a small, lonesome place at the verge of a hill in a secluded mountain valley. And there was a lake. That lake had been my secret pride when I was little and all by myself in Seoul attending school. It was the one thing, my one and only trump card, that I could shout out in my mind when those brats in Seoul got to teasing me. *You know what? We have a lake at our orchard in the country—a lake!* I pronounced "lake" with a great deal of pride, because there was a face that always followed in its wake as soon as I uttered that magical word, and there was a secret love I had received from the owner of that face, a clumsy love I felt to be almost unconditional, a love that lasted because it was clumsy.

I learned early on that not all that has vanished is beautiful. Throughout my life—or half of it, at least—I learned it through Uncle Chŏng, the handyman at the desolate orchard my parents had acquired in the countryside with much difficulty. He referred to himself as Ajaebi, a humble, avuncular appellation, and that is how he was known to all. Both the orchard and Ajaebi are gone now. For a long time I shut the memory of his life out of my mind. He passed away early, barely beyond his mid-fifties, and to settle the debts that had accumulated over time we were forced to sell the orchard just before my daughter was born. In its place there is now an inn resembling a hillside villa; no trace of the orchard remains. He's gone and the orchard too, and the lake has been filled in with dirt. And what I am left with is one thing alone—an overwhelming sorrow. The sorrow of one who has never repaid even a measure of the great love she has received, who just when she's become faintly aware of her gains and losses in life and attempts to repay that love, realizes that the object of her indebtedness is gone. The sorrow that fills her heart at that instant is like water filling a well. And whenever it wells up, I have a mad desire to speak endlessly of the debt of love that was once my pride and the lake that is a small symbol of that love.

But I have never told anyone my story, all of it, to its conclusion. Not even my husband. He too grieved when we sold the orchard that had meant so much to me, not as much as I but still enough to comfort me. And back when we had started dating, he had already heard enough about the orchard handyman, who had long since passed on. But to tell all about a person's life to someone who never knew him is troubling work, indeed an impossible task for one who lacks the patience to explain everything step by step. Worse, because my listener, however empathic he might be, does not share my emotional twists and turns, he is likely to feel left out. For this or whatever other reason, my stories invariably came out stale and bland. There were times when I thought I had related the entire tale, only to feel the next instant an emptiness both unexpected and bewildering.

Even before I became aware of it, because of a slight movement of the curtains or the shadows cast by flowering plants—frequently it was something quite insignificant—the old sorrow would well up from my heart, choking me. The story of the orchard and of Ajaebi, in what tone of voice should I tell it? Should I tell it in whispers, as if revealing with great reluctance something hidden and taboo? Should I tell it breathlessly, exaggerating like we do when we're talking about a person with whom we have no direct connection? Or perhaps the tone should be offhand and frivolous, as when we say, "How horrible," but don't really mean it? I guess I could highlight the anecdotes in a more tragic tone—in a way that might come closest to the reality—but the strange thing is, the melancholy I feel won't let me do that, because I'm afraid that the tragedy in my voice would destroy the words and make them disappear.

"Mama, I've finished my picture diary."

"Let's have a look. . . . Well, this doesn't look like a diary to me. There's no ocean, no yachts where we are now. Why don't you just draw the ducks and the turkey?"

"Mama, I'm tired."

"Then how about I tell you a story—a story that happened a long, long time ago?"

"A true story or one that's made up?"

"A true story, of course."

"You mean that story about when you lived in the country? Mama, you're so old-fashioned."

"All right, then, you can go play instead."

As if freed from an onerous curfew, she picked up the dragonfly net that was leaning against a tree and ran off toward the house. Her mind had already zeroed in on the backyard, where flowering trees were in bloom and where in a thriving tangle of weeds the dragonflies had their stronghold.

My child, why don't people grow up sooner? That you are still a child wears me out so. Yes, my child, I'll tell you the story you're fond of, the story about the bicycle. I wonder if you remember all the stories I whispered to you before you were born. Stories innumerable that I whispered while I waited for you. You were fond of the bicycle story and the lake story. Do you remember? When I felt you grumbling inside me and I told you the lake or the bicycle story, you became still. Yes, there was a bicycle, a magic bicycle. I don't remember when my eyes and my body got so used to it, but the bicycle became like another two legs attached to my own. My child, look over there, in the shadows of distant time—that bicycle leaning against the stump. Do you see it? Ah, of course the air in the tires is taking a rest, the chain and the leather seat are discolored, the spring beneath the seat is rusted. But no matter. To be at rest is to loosen, grow slack. . . . Still, my child, imagine that bicycle with a basket on the carrying rack, the old tires pumped full of air and shedding their dust, the wheel spokes whirling, the chain oiled. . . . Imagine it speeding through the secret shaded places of the orchard. . . . My child, nobody can touch the bicycle resting in the shade. If you touch it, it just might crumble into dust.

On the day the lake came into being in the orchard, I knew that you too would someday come into being. I must have been about one and a half times your age now. At the end of that year's awe-

*some monsoons, a large water hole was hollowed out. The lake
came into being a few days later. It was Ajaebi's gift. Yes, my child,
after he dug for three days and three nights in the large water hole
made by the long rainy season and captured the water streaming
down the hillside, the lake came into being.*

There are times when, quite unexpectedly, we become witness to someone else's life. Like the other evening, when I saw
something that ought to have remained unseen. On that cool
early summer evening I had gone out to the walkway fronting
our apartment building and was looking absently at the building opposite, waiting for our daughter to come back from her
friend's. Since ours is a crowded apartment complex, the inte-
riors of the apartments across the way, less than fifty yards off,
were clearly visible. My absent gaze was caught by something:
a man and a woman grappling over a knife—a large kitchen
knife, there was no mistaking it—a horribly chaotic scene that
was clearly visible against the background of the lighted interior. The scene—more exaggerated, surreal even, because their
voices were inaudible—was like something out of a violent
film. Quieting my pounding heart, I went to the door of what
I thought was their apartment and strained to listen. No sound
came from within. There was only a stream of words from a
television blaring from the open door of the next apartment,
but the voices sounded as stereo in my mind.

There was nothing I could do. I felt strangely impotent,
which always makes me mutter to myself, "What a fool I am."
But in this case my inaction turned out to have been the correct
thing. On the weekend a few days later, when the knife-wielding
couple passed by me, smiling, their arms linked together affec-
tionately, all I could do was walk by them quickly with my eyes
downcast so I wouldn't stare at the bruise on the woman's face.
I can't count all the times such things have happened to me.
Things everyone else would soon forget, considering them

unimportant, yet they destroy the tranquility of my everyday life each time they happen. How frightful it is to witness the hidden lives of others! I had come to understand early in life that to be such a witness is to incur a debt that will follow you around all your life. And that was when I asked myself, without really understanding what I was asking, "Did Ajaebi love me because he chose me to be the witness to his life, or did he choose me because he loved me?"

Only later, much, much later, when I began to uncover the links essential to understanding his life, did I ask myself a different question: "What did he wish for when he chose me as his witness?"

Our daughter is now eight years old; in no time she'll be ten! After capturing three or four dragonflies, which she proceeded to imprison in her yellow plastic dragonfly house, she looked like she was going to be prancing around in my vicinity for a while, but now I couldn't see her. I wondered if she had gone inside for a nap. Maybe it's because we had our daughter almost in our mid-thirties that our vacation plans, right down to the packing of our bags, always turned into a big production. We wanted to make it the kind of vacation she would remember all her life. Playing at being an American Indian, or a firefighter. . . . Not long ago her dream was to be a firefighter wearing a red helmet. Now her dream is to be an assassin infiltrating an extraterrestrial world.

Different from our grand plan, as soon as my husband rose he left for his fishing hole in a village off beyond the orchard. Why didn't I dislike him, this maniac for fishing? I liked to visualize him beneath the scorching sun, sitting at his fishing hole after throwing in his line. It was like we were each playing at a secret game we alone knew. When he returned in the evening and put down his creel, empty except for a few still-wiggling loach, I loved seeing his face with such a purified look. Yes, I like people who know how to sit for a long time in front of water. For I know it's not something just anyone can enjoy. After lunch together my daughter and I sat on a mat spread out in a corner of the orchard and I tried half-heartedly to play along in a game she had suggested, but my thoughts insisted on wandering the orchard and lake of my long-ago childhood.

I don't know by what course of events my parents, originally from Songnim in Hwanghae Province, came to own the orchard that became their livelihood. I vaguely remember hearing that they might have been helped a great deal by someone from their ancestral village who had come south earlier and grown wealthy. My parents, innocent beginners in life when they had lived in the North, came south all by themselves and settled down to a life of farming, in which they had little experience. They cleared hillsides into dry fields and they planted fruit trees. Still, I don't remember them ever being well off. They named their orchard—and me—Songnim, or Pine Forest, after the ancestral village, though there weren't many pine trees on our Songnim Farm. Perhaps because the work of the orchard was too much for my inexperienced parents, my father had frequent bouts of sickness from early on. How much more desperate the situation would have been if on a certain night a certain man had not arrived to live at the orchard. If not for that man's helping hand, the orchard would have reverted to its earlier state, a wilder, uncultivated hillside. As it did after that man was dead and gone.

That young man was Ajaebi, and he spent the difficult latter half of his life with my parents as the orchard handyman. But I don't remember him ever being young. Because he called my mother Older Sister and my father Older Brother, I thought he was a relative. In time I heard he was a former

POW, an anti-Communist who at our orchard had found a
new life. According to what I overheard my parents say when
I was a child, he had been found unconscious and wracked
with fever at the foot of the hill. Luckily my father was the
first to see him. In two weeks' time he was healthy again, and
before long he became known to the village people as one of
my parents' distant relatives. Since what I call our village con-
sisted of no more than twenty households in a remote mountain valley, it was almost as if Ajaebi had dropped out of the
sky and into our orchard. When the village people talked
about him, the word "POW" would slip out now and then,
dark and sinister. But I soon forgot that darkness, because I
could not reconcile it with the bright smile that lit up his eyes
whenever he looked at me. And the others too must have forgotten that word as they came to know him as the person who
single-handedly took on all the difficult work of the village.
In this way, coming to our orchard at about the time of my
birth and becoming one of our family, he became indispensable not only to us but also to the village people. A relative
who didn't speak the amusing and affectionate northern dia-
lect my parents used and who worked in silence the whole
day long. Such was what I understood of him when I was
little.

Because of Father's chronic illness and Mother's having to
nurse him as well as do the physical labor around the house,
I have a lot more memories of time spent with Ajaebi than
with my parents. I played baby games with him, sitting on
his knee; I learned to read from him before starting elementary school. Taking me to and from school, a mile and a half
away, was also his responsibility, as was looking over my
homework with me sitting beside him, as I'm doing now
with my daughter, and telling me ghost and goblin stories in
a slow and halting manner, deliberately mimicking an old

man. The orchard was his, at least in the sense that his hands were the means by which everything there was accomplished. As soon as school was over, I would follow him around, learning how to prune trees and plant flower seeds. One summer vacation he made a tree house for me out of thin planks, and there I sat and played. When the weather was good, he would sneak food from the pantry for our fishing trips—food that Mother was saving for the ritual birthday ceremonies for Grandfather and Grandmother, left behind in the North. They were delicious happenings, delicious enough to have nearly erased any memory of deprivation. Thus I reached the age of ten following him around, heart and soul.

The day I turned ten, Ajaebi had a meeting arranged by a matchmaker. He had been refusing to consider marriage, even though he was by then in his late thirties. Did he suddenly give in that one time to my mother's insistence, or did he merely go along with it? He took me with him to meet the woman, who worked at a soup-and-rice place in a town some six miles off. The dirt road over the mountain pass seemed unusually bleached out and endless that day. For me who had been roughing it at the orchard like a feral beast, it was a genuinely curious experience, enough so that I could vividly recount all the details. Additionally, the dark interior of the soup-and-rice place; the old woman with the moustache under her nose just like a man's, the likes of whom I had never seen in my life; and the melancholy faces of a man and a woman, mouths clamped shut, the old hag sitting between them, puffing on a cigarette and continually filling Ajaebi's drinking vessel—all these established in my mind a fixed bias against the so-called matchmaking meeting. It took root in my consciousness, accompanied by enough stink and gloom to chill my heart.

It was on this very day that I became for the first time a witness to his life. The decisive moment came—if we were to look at its effect—when he asked me on our way back, "Song-a, dear, you saw her. How did she look to you?"

Maybe it was because his face was flushed from drink—and he wasn't used to drinking. When he looked at me with an unusually bright gaze, I knew this was no time to play games or to lie. "She didn't look like she could live at our orchard. Right?"

My answer arose from my very real concern that if this match were to take place, he might leave the orchard forever and go to live at the soup-and-rice place with the sorrowful-looking woman who wasn't even pretty.

He didn't say anything for quite some time. By then the town was behind us and we were walking along the bleached-out dirt road. I remember it was spring, because he made me a flute with a twig broken off a flowering tree.

"Yes, Song-a, you're right. Most likely she won't be able to live with me. Anyway, Ajaebi has a son. And besides, since my wife is alive and well, how could I get married again? It's foolish."

"If it's your son, Ajaebi, then isn't he my brother? Where is he? Can I bring him home with us?"

"No, Song-a, you couldn't bring him home even if you knew where he was."

"Wow, Ajaebi, I think you made that up."

"Yes, Song-a, I made up a story and I'm being a tease. I don't even know why I said that."

Still, the woman from the soup-and-rice place came to live at the orchard. And then one night she left—left without even taking her things. She had been with us for six months. That she stole away from the orchard was perfectly understandable. After she arrived, Ajaebi accompanied me to school more frequently, coming back long before school was out to wait for me by the playground, smoking. By then I was feeling all grown up, so I considered Ajaebi a nuisance because if I went home with him, I couldn't play with my friends after school. After the woman arrived, he would remain longer and later at our place than at the little cottage at the foot of the hill that he had built for himself and her. And more frequently he and Father would play chess until very late, and as they had always done the two of them would talk endlessly together, and he would sometimes fall asleep on the wooden floor of the veranda outside our family room. And whenever he and the woman were alone, he would come for me and have me sit with them like a hostage in order to escape the awkwardness and stiffness between them. As the days passed, the undercurrent of deep, gloomy silence wore increasingly on my nerves, finally making me bolt whenever he summoned me. It was at this point that the woman vanished.

I have often thought that I was responsible for the woman's flight, that the gap between Ajaebi and the woman became wider because of what I said on our way back from the matchmaking meeting. But as I grew older and discovered more about him, and as I looked back on their brief life together, the only conclusion I could draw was that what happened to them had been unavoidable, and no one could have done anything about it. For, to put it in a sentence, he was in a different place entirely.

My child, I feel dizzy. Sometimes I am greatly distressed because I fear I have brought you into an unsafe world. Although some have suggested I try the so-called mind control or zen, I wonder if I am not an offspring of a reptile family. Because I feel most comfortable when I am crawling on the ground. My child, if I had a chance to start over again, I think I would first change how we measure things. For sure. I would measure all distances and heights by drops of sweat. Mount Paektu, Mount Halla, Mount Chiri. . . . Mountains like these would be measured by 500, 400, 300 drops of sweat per yard above sea level, and from Chongno to Seoul Station 50 drops of sweat per yard, and so on. Work would also be measured by sweat. Work of 400 drops of sweat per hour and work of 500 drops of sweat per hour. Measured this way, the lake into which Ajaebi put the sky on a certain day, how many drops of sweat would it be worth? And I wonder . . . what if we could convert all the tears we shed in our lives into energy? The energy of one teardrop. . . . What should be the conversion rate for the energy of our tears? Just call it drops of . . . ? Like, for instance, tears worth five drops of energy. Such a pointless game allows us to forget the frightful holes we see when the ground suddenly splits open.

I can't help smiling when I think about your beginning. I thought there surely would be a peal of thunder and my body would radiate bright light. Such signs would show themselves everywhere in me, letting the whole world know. But you came quietly without a sound, without a sign. Two months inside my belly before you announced yourself. So secret and so shy you were.

My child, you who are without the energy of tears, you whose tears cannot yet be converted into energy. What stories shall I tell you now, stories that are not whisperings inside the belly?

I never saw Ajaebi shed tears. But the strange thing is, when I think of his aged countenance, what comes to mind is a wrinkled and tearful face—perhaps because I alone knew of the several times when he might actually have wanted to cry. That face of his then was the face I disliked the most, the face that made me most angry. Upon reflection, it occurs to me that I rarely saw on his face the shimmering smile that reminds me of springtime heat. To the village people, the orchard handyman was only a reticent, melancholy man of small stature, albeit a workman extraordinaire.

I knew—though I don't know precisely *when* I first knew—that he was neither a former anti-Communist POW nor a native of my parents' ancestral village, only that he had escaped from somewhere. I didn't learn this from my parents or from the villagers with whom we had the most contact. But whether it was intuition or the exercise of my imagination triggered by some ambiguous clue he happened to drop when we were alone, I came to understand he had been a fugitive. From what precisely, I never knew. It seemed such a grave matter, I dared not ask about it.

When I was thirteen, I became for the second time a witness to his life, a witness who could only conclude he was a fugitive, with all the privations that entailed. The small event that occurred in the summer of that year could have been related to my leaving home for Seoul. For it was he who expressed the deepest regret—grief even—at my leaving to go to school there. To me his expression of regret and grief was the most natural thing. Young as I was, I took his expression of love for me as a kind of bonus, something I deserved above and beyond the love of my parents.

I made several trips to Seoul with Mother to apply to a girls' middle school, now that I had finished elementary school back home. My parents had no relatives in Seoul—they had come from the North all by themselves—so Mother and I spent a couple of weeks at an inn, until we decided on a boardinghouse for me. Leaving me by myself in our shabby room at the inn to prepare for the entrance examination, Mother ran around Seoul from dawn till late at night. She had already decided I would pass the exam as a matter of course, but even after she found a boardinghouse not far from the school, she continued to spend entire days going around the city. Clearly her attention was taken up with something other than my entrance exam. And it could not have been simply the curiosity of someone who was a stranger to Seoul, for she wore the same peculiar expression she sometimes displayed when she talked about the family and the landmarks she had left behind in her ancestral village, an expression equally of excitement and blankness. A similarly misty expression had doubtless veiled my face as well when my husband made his proposal about taking care of his friend's orchard. Looking at Mother's face late one night when she returned to the inn, I knew immediately she had found whatever it was she had sought.

As soon as we learned I had passed the entrance exam, Mother hurried back to the orchard to catch up on housework. I had no problem adjusting to Seoul, maybe because I had inherited from my parents the toughness of Hwanghae people. I would astonish my classmates by doing wild, eccentric things like running barefoot out onto the playground when it rained; lifting effortlessly the flower pots no one else could lift in the gardening class; and reviving in one week an all but dead flowerbed. Although I was summoned now and then to the school counselor's room because of my loud wailing and laughing in the empty after-hours classroom, I managed quite well in my own way.

"Father is unwell, come home this weekend. And don't forget to buy such-and-such medications and bring them with you." Rather than such letters from my parents, I much preferred Ajaebi's succinct missives: "In your absence even the grass is withering—Ajaebi." Letters that had me mumbling to myself, "Ajaebi is a poet."

My first summer break from school in Seoul arrived. I was now thirteen. It was during that summer break that my father's chronic heart disease turned decisively worse. Ajaebi's nursing of Father was even more devoted than Mother's, which continued unchanged in its intensity or tenderness to the very last. Any change? Unthinkable! Better than brothers born of the same mother, each understanding the other by glances alone, they became practically inseparable. Several times late at night I saw Ajaebi scribbling and erasing in old notebooks I no longer kept. That I became particularly interested in these notebooks only belatedly might have been because I too had begun to keep a journal around then. For all I know, he might have been writing in notebooks for quite a long time.

Whenever there was a pause in the work of the orchard, Ajaebi would come running to Father for one of their low, whispered conversations. It seemed to me that for the most part he talked with Father about matters related to the orchard. They would speak in hushed voices for the longest time. When Father had been able to move about with ease, they used to sit together on the wooden bench in front of the house. But after Father's condition worsened, they closeted themselves in the room where Father's bedding was spread out. When they were thus engrossed, it was understood no one was to disturb them; Mother was to sleep in my room or in the room across from Father's, because they would talk through the night. Their whisperings, coming seemingly from afar, sounded so peaceful that even recalling them evoked in me a sharp and aching longing for them.

At the end of that same summer there occurred a strange journey. Ajaebi, as he often did, wanted to take me into town to get Father's medications and look at new and improved insecticides and farm implements, and it was perfectly sensible for him to want someone along to help him bring everything back. But as soon as we got into town that day, he hurried through the errands. And then, leaving our purchases at the farm machinery store, but without a word of explanation, he took me onto a bus with him. Two hours over country roads,

off the bus for a quick lunch, then back on. Something fierce
about him prevented me from asking myself why I followed
him so unquestioningly, and the face gazing fixedly outside
the window was too icy and forbidding for me to question
him. I ended up falling asleep inside that sultry bus without
exchanging a single word with him.

The place where we arrived as the sun was slanting past its
meridian was a small town not far from M City. We went into
a snow cone shop near the depot. Only then did I notice that
Ajaebi was advancing toward the fringes of old age. He was
by then barely forty. I saw traces of tears beneath the eyes of
that prematurely aged face. With folded arms he was pressing
down hard on his chest, as if by doing so he might hold his
aching heart in check. In a strained voice he ordered two of
my favorite sweet buns and a glass of crushed ice mixed with
sweet beans. I grew anxious watching the flies flitting about
madly inside. Ajaebi himself touched none of the things he
had ordered.

He was not the only one unable to outrun time. I too had
reached a certain age: I was too embarrassed to play the baby
or make him laugh by saying something totally absurd. And
it was I who started sobbing quietly. Waking from an uneasy
sleep, finding us in a strange town, I was overcome by the
thought that I was an utter failure in helping Ajaebi in his
desperate effort at self-control. There was also a feeling of
lonesomeness produced by the fading light of the waning day.
But more than anything else, I was afraid I would prove incapable when he finally put to me the task for which we
had come such a long distance. If there was ever a time when I
so regretted my immaturity as a child, I can't remember it.
Had I been a grown-up, I would have found the appropriate
words to ease his feeling of helplessness, instantly lifting the
gloom from his face by a miracle wrought with a grown-up's

wisdom—or so I had thought at the time. But how is it now that I am a grown-up? Recalling how I used to think back then will occasionally bring a wry smile to my face. For if I were to face the same events now as an adult, no doubt I would have tasted, as I did then, the same shocked confusion of utter helplessness. There are sorrows that cannot be eased.

"Song-a, there's something I want you to do, and it's very simple. You can do it, I know you can. All you have to do is toss this inside the gate when no one's looking, that's all. Nothing's going to happen."

As he said this he slid a ticket-shaped letter into my handbag on the table, a letter he had shaped by folding a half sheet of notebook paper lengthwise, then twisting it three times so the top and bottom corners folded into each other. He then produced a sheet of paper and explained in a whisper that on it was the address and a rough sketch of the house I had to find. For an instant the image of Mother back then in Seoul, tramping around the city and copying something down after returning late to the inn, superimposed itself upon the address of the house. And then I understood—Ajaebi was doing something against my mother's wishes; in handing me this rough sketch, he was going against what he had promised not to do.

He went over the steps again and again until the directions began to sound automatic: find the house, wait till no one was around, drop the letter inside the gate. What lay before me seemed like a journey to the country of death. Vaguely afraid that a mistake in carrying out the task might imperil not only Ajaebi but also my family, I was trembling as I left the snow cone shop. Along the way I must have asked about the name of the district, the location of the post office, and the way to the rear gate of the elementary school; I must have encountered people as I went along—people and faces impossible to remember now. Rushing around in confusion, having lost my bearings on a street that stretched out in a straight line, I felt exactly like I did trying to follow a road in a nightmare. As I approached the house, though, I regained a degree of cool-headedness that surprised me. To quiet my wildly beating heart I entered the playground of the elementary school—the final obstacle to my destination. A hot wind swirled around a lonesome playground vacated by school-children on summer break. I was all alone. To understand the nature of the task I was performing, I took the ticket-shaped letter from my handbag, unfolded it, and spread it out. The familiar longish strokes of Ajaebi's handwriting appeared: "No time for the moon to rise on the water of the stream."

A sentence without head or tail. A message that made no sense. I turned over the sheet, but there was nothing else. The deserted playground seemed an infinite expanse, and I was terrified.

In the end, dropping the letter through a gap in the closed gate of the isolated house was not so difficult. It was as Ajaebi had said. Arriving at the ill-fitting gate, I peered into the shabby-looking cement-layered courtyard but saw no one. How could I fail to do this much for Ajaebi! I must have steeled myself with such thoughts. In went the letter.

I jumped up. A faint voice had called out, a slightly hoarse voice saying something like "Song-a." Then I realized the voice was for my inattentive ears, and yes, it must have been calling me for some time. A child's voice calling "Mama," and not my name, Song-a. I looked around, feeling only the high noon's heat surrounding me like a wall of fire—nothing came into view. On the mat were my daughter's bag with her summer vacation homework, the picture diary with the sea, the many-colored crayons smooth and shiny, looking like they were about to melt. I looked wildly in all directions. My hair stood on end and I broke out in a sweat.

She wasn't there!

I tried to call her, but my voice stuck in my throat. I ran toward where I thought the faint voice had come from. I couldn't hear it now. The only sound was the incongruous squawk of the turkey a short distance off. I went inside, looked into every room, found only dark, cool silence. Like a madwoman I ran through the ground floor, the basement, and the storage room calling her name. I flew out of the house thinking how ghastly and disheveled I must look, ran to the backyard where I had last seen her with her dragonfly net. I shouted insanely, "Ŭn-ha! Ŭn-ha-*ya*!" And finally I heard the faint, reedy voice calling "Mama." But when I turned in the direction of the voice I could see nothing. *Maybe the front yard!* I ran there, backpedaled away from the house, and looked up. There she was, up on the roof, where the sun's scorching heat was beating down, face daubed in black crayon, not daring to move, fixed to the spot. I felt like my blood had evaporated. With a supreme effort I managed to control my voice. The girl, though fearful, was sitting smartly astride the ridge of the roof, as if riding a horse. I remembered there was a ladder out back. She must have climbed that ladder onto the roof. I mustered just enough energy to say prayerfully, "My child, what are doing up there?"

The image of our daughter falling from the roof and writhing on the ground flashed through my mind. She stared at me in silence, evidently surprised at my calm façade.

"You need to come down right now. You don't want to get sunstroke, do you?"

Eyes tightly shut, I slowly turned away from the frightful scene. She called out to me, her voice urgent. I turned back to see her small hands reaching out toward me.

"Since you climbed up there all by yourself, shouldn't you climb down by yourself? Mama will stay right here while you climb down nice and slow and careful."

I imagined a fiery sparkle in her pretty eyes. She started to move. Cautiously. Like a cat, first one step, then two. Yes, that's it. That's my girl. Yes, just like that. *Ŭn-ha-ya*, I shouted in my mind, *for you it's that easy!* Finally, her face disappeared from the roof, and a short while later she ran to me from the back of the house. That brief interval felt like eternity.

I embraced her small, hot body as hard as I could. Only then, freeing herself from my embrace, did she run to the shade, sit, and burst into plaintive tears. In the emptiness of the orchard her cries reverberated.

"You look like a chimney ghost. Come to Mama. I'll give you a bath."

"What for, when you hate me so, Mother!"

She spoke formally when she was resentful. Violently shaking her head, she resumed her crying, which before long became a wail.

"If you keep on crying like that, the turkey will run up to you thinking you're her sister. Come—come here."

She looked like she wanted to laugh, but stubbornly she shook her head again.

"What for, you hate me so, Mother!"

I went close and held her tightly. She squirmed like a fish.

"Don't you know how much Mama loves our Ŭn-ha. More than love. Mama *respects* her."

Over and over I kissed her cheeks and the crown of her head, hot to the touch. Long enough until her sorrow melted away. Until her squirming gradually ceased and she yielded her small body gently to my embrace.

"Respect is better than love, right, Mama?"

"Not better. But heavier and deeper."

"Mama, why do you respect me?"

"Because you don't yet have the energy of tears. And because you came down safely from the roof."

"What's the energy of tears?"

"Well, I wonder sometimes."

I took her to where the faucet was and picked up the long hose lying among the still-small garden plants. I opened the faucet all the way. The strong gush of water was like a shout of joy. I turned the hose on her baby-chubby naked body caked with dust and dirt.

This child, who is like a rose moss with its small plump leaves.

My child, you who are still without the energy of tears, you who still live in the country of poets, you who are like Mozart and van Gogh, what shall I do with you? I just want to crush you in my arms. My child, I like it when you do crazy things. Like coming home with your feet bruised from playing jump rope; like when you wailed for more than five hours like a pig getting its throat cut because you wouldn't accept my unfairness; when you never give in and ask for forgiveness; when you threw all your toys out the window in a tantrum because you didn't want to go to school; when you put a doll in your place and ran away like the wind just as I was about to punish you by having you stand with your hands raised high like tree branches. It's at those times I like you the most.

We had ourselves a delightful time playing in the water and acting silly. We returned dripping wet to our mat in the shade and she sat quietly, chin on her knees and wearing the prettiest expression. When she was little she sometimes awakened before we did, and looking up toward the window she would quietly regard the dawn light streaming in. Her face as I awoke to discover it then was the face of a philosopher. Impulsively I drew her to me in an embrace, and turned the page of her picture diary. With a blank page before me, I picked up a half-melted blue crayon. She looked up at me, her interest aroused.

"Mama, draw Ulysses. And Argos!"

Ulysses and his loyal dog Argos seemed to have been transformed into a righteous assassin and his partner in the comics she read. I drew a circle.

"Ha, what's this?" she asked, eyes wide open, gently biting her lip. She seemed perfectly content now that she was in her mama's embrace, with an expression that always made me smile. But her eyes were already misting over with sleep.

"What do you think? Try and guess."

"The sky?"

"Possibly. What else?"

She drew invisible lines with her finger below and beside the circle, making up the syllables *ŭn* and *ha*.

"Since it's Ŭn-ha if I do this, it's my name. Right?"

"Yes indeed. And what else? Close your eyes and think. This is a lake. And also a bicycle wheel."

She gently shut her eyes, her expression thoughtful. And she said, as if she was trying to be kind, "Mama, please tell me the story about the house in the country long ago."

"All right, but you have to promise not to open your eyes. . . . Think of a lake that's round. And also a bicycle with two round wheels whirling in furious circles. In the village where I lived at your age, there was a forest where a lot of tree families lived together, and also a lake where every morning the trees could see their reflections as they washed themselves. On the surface of the lake slim girl insects called water striders swam the whole day long, and in the evening kingfishers swooped and soared above the water searching for their dinner . . ."

The weight of her head came to rest on my chest. Released from her tension, she had fallen asleep.

My child, it's a war out there. Always a war, whatever the year, whatever the hour, whichever the continent. No matter how hard you try to escape it, and whatever defenses you put up, the smell of war seeps through the cracks in every door—you can't hide from it. It's a horrible smell, hard and sticky, and it cuts up the world in straight lines. I wish I could change all the ugly words in the world for your sake. . . . I wish I could give airlike lightness and softness to all the hard muscle-bound words, and exchange all the stinking words for the names of wildflowers: pearlweed, sengreen, wild rose, goosefoot, veronica, buttercup, kirilow indigo, squill, fern acacia, fringed pink, aster, and this one—rose moss, yes, rose moss. . . . My child, you must somehow become a poet who turns ugly words into beautiful ones, stench into fragrance, from whose mouth flows music. . . . You must become a classical poet through and through. You know how to make words like "toe," "peanut," and "snot" sound beautiful. When you were learning how to write, you wrote your family name, 박, crookedly—you said the word was laughing. The stink that seeps into this faraway orchard's stagnant waste water, please get rid of it quickly, my child. Your smile is a very strong, very fragrant deodorizer. My child, who can smile so radiantly, you might be from another world. That's why as soon as you get on the bicycle and start moving forward, pedaling fast with your short thin legs like the water strider, I feel my chest start to pound. I see your bicycle accelerating, the front wheel lifting into the air, soaring higher and higher.

The old notebooks he left behind were filled with incomprehensible scribblings too formal to be diary entries, and among them were a considerable number of neatly aligned but cryptic passages like this one:

A small lake is there. All around the lake I planted rose moss.

When will all the dots on the calendar become stars?

Flesh, love, people, livelihood, white frost, frost pattern, have a good life. . . .

Several of these coded passages were transferred to single notebook pages, and once every few years they were folded into ticket-shaped letters. Written always in longish strokes. Ticket-shaped letters always folded three times. Well, maybe they weren't all coded messages.

Five times all told over the course of ten years or more, from the first journey to the last before his death, I delivered his odd letters. The recipients were his wife and son, three or four years older than I. But I did not learn these things from what he said to me. There is such a thing as knowledge before explanation, that which is too obvious. Besides, during that decade between the first and the fifth delivery I gained enough composure to be curious about the recipients. Never again did I experience the kind of vertigo I had felt in front of the first house, which had made everything go blank before my eyes, the house in the vicinity of M City with its old slate roof falling in. And never again did I, as I had the first time, prowl about the house before throwing the letter into the yard and running away. Once I saw them through a crack in the gate, saw them from behind. And I couldn't forget it—that wasn't how you should look at somebody.

Each of the five deliveries, the address was different. I don't know how he managed to find the new address when the family moved. Let's assume Mother had found the first address by asking around. What about the next one? Our journey when I was thirteen, whatever untold secret my parents had guessed from our late-night return. . . . I do not remember Father, Mother, and Ajaebi sleeping that night. My parents scolded him long and hard—a verbal rebuke, not a quarrel—and Ajaebi must have kept his silence throughout, because I did not hear his voice. I fell asleep in my dark room trying to follow the irregular, changing images flickering behind my closed eyes.

I never did find out what promise he made in response to my parents' tearful appeal, but in any case my courier duty would resume just when I had almost forgotten it. This is something I've never revealed to anyone.

For a long time I thought his cryptic odes to nature might be coded messages. An ingenious method of communication devised for himself and the recipients when unavoidable circumstances had compelled them to part. Some time later, when I became better acquainted with the details of Ajaebi's life, I discovered that the importance of the letters was simply to let the family know he was alive; a faint signal that he was, albeit from afar, functioning as a sort of lighthouse keeper, transmitting a beacon generated by despair. But since he did not or could not show his face, ever, he was a lighthouse keeper the family could not accept. How anachronistic life sometimes seems! For by the time I had decided I could not tolerate the situation, he had passed on to the next world.

The third letter I delivered to an address in Seoul. From a very small hilltop house with a half basement on the outskirts of a town, to another small but somewhat better home, and from there to a slightly larger house in the traditional style— although the houses I knew were only of these three types, the family had moved several times over a period of ten years. . . . And one evening very much later, several seasons after his death, in a sudden fit I ran breathlessly to the house where I had delivered the last of the letters. I cast off all the customary precautions—looking to see if anyone might be watching, surveying the surroundings, worrying about any potential harm to his family—for the purpose of conveying to them the clamoring voices within me. Determined simply to create an incident. Belatedly.

They were no longer there. At the district office I learned that the son's name had been removed from the list of registered residents. The reason? "Gone overseas." The wife's name remained, with no indication that her residence had changed. In any event, neither of them could be seen in the house where they used to live. In their place were a young couple with a child, just like us, and they appeared quite happy. They said that when they first came looking to rent as well as when they moved in, they saw no one except the owner, certainly no renters, and the day they moved in, the house was vacant. The best they could do for me was to jot down the owner's address. No further did I pursue the whereabouts of Ajaebi's family, in accordance with Ajaebi's own example. As a show of minimum courtesy in respect of their tragically wasted past.

My child, when will people all grow up to be as big as you? Your forehead seems so broad and deep. Like the small lake, the lake bordered all around with blooming rose moss. I feel a thirst when I am looking at you. My child, let's walk out onto that road. I shouldn't be like this, but whenever you are asleep, child, I want to shake you awake. And to chatter on and on. Yes, while all those people of long ago were sleeping peacefully, a crack appeared in the earth. . . . That's today's story, which has become an old story. Ah, my child, I have not yet found the way. How shall I tell the story? Should it be the story of a storm? The story of a light spring rain? Or maybe it should be the story of the hot summer sun that's beating down like it is now?

He was a fugitive. A death sentence awaited him. He was a high-ranking official, a member of the Workers Party in the South. He was in hiding, awaiting his chance to escape to the North. He was arrested in transit. Miraculously he escaped—even though the guards had taken his clothes and personal effects to prevent that very possibility. He had fled on the back of a dark night as on the back of a horse. Into an orchard. Forever.

Such were the details I heard from my exhausted mother when I went home to attend Father's funeral and then Ajaebi's, the details spilling almost unconsciously from her mouth like a shaman's chant. Perhaps it was because of my unbearable grief at having lost him, but in this history I had learned belatedly, I found an excuse to hate him. What kind of grand escape had I expected? A fool, a dullard, a coward, a cowardly fugitive. I resented having been chosen to witness the life of such a pitiable person. I blamed him as if he had prevented me from speaking with his wife and son, whom I had so wanted to meet, when actually I myself was to blame, infected by that insidious history that had oppressed his life. It was something effected by my twisted emotions. I was mad with resentment that although I had been the carrier of his messages, I had not shouted out even once, "Your husband, your father lives at the foot of that hill over there!" Hating him so passionately, it seemed, I could gradually ease my sorrow. Fortunately, my hatred did not last long.

Some time later I went home to sell the orchard, which by then had reverted to an overgrown hillside. There were insufficient hands to work it, but more important was our need to sell it to pay off the debts connected with Father's long illness. Three or four workmen were already at the orchard constructing a retaining wall. My daughter would be born shortly.

Sitting by the lake, where I could look out at the road stretching in a straight line from the orchard, I viewed with loving attention every detail of this familiar landscape that I might never see again. Although it had not been kept up, to me it was peace, even if it were to vanish one day. The trees, silent partners, knowing all that had happened at the orchard, indifferent to any worries that might come tomorrow, were like a network of tiny veins etched against the blue sky. The trees had shed their leaves with the coming of fall.

In my mind there appears an image—Father taking a short walk on that deserted road, laboring, his hand resting on Ajaebi's shoulder, and Ajaebi next to Father, looking like his shadow. Just the two of them. I've always thought they looked most beautiful at such times. What did they have to talk about? Father, when he was young and healthy, used to make anti-Communist speeches in town and at my elementary school. Father, who had chosen to come south all alone, leaving his family behind in the North. The people in the audience would nod their heads in approval, making me feel proud of him.

It was Father who had found Ajaebi in the orchard, a man who had once been a dedicated official of the Workers Party in the South. And Father had protected him from danger, becoming his lifelong sworn brother. And in Ajaebi's notebooks that Mother gave me there was much more than writings in praise of nature. Those notebooks were filled with—though the handwriting was often illegible—the thoughts, incoherent as they were, to which he had clung all his life, and the threads connecting all that had happened to him. He seems to have lived his life unreformed, and not to have concealed any of it from Father or Mother. Many events inexplicable by common sense alone seem to have occurred before he came into their lives and after he departed, and those events stayed with them.

I heard their whisperings everywhere in the orchard. Was it the fundamental differences between them that prompted their endless whisperings? Especially late at night on the bench in front of the house, in the narrow paths of the orchard, in the vicinity of the lake at the foot of the hill. . . . All I had to do was listen, and I could hear them whispering like the wind. Especially at the lake. That whispering is what makes me remember, bringing a gentle smile to my face, even now after so many years, our bleak and difficult life at the orchard.

Another image: How old was I then—twenty-six? twenty-seven? It was summertime, as it always is in these images, and the weekend—and my vacation at the orchard—had come to an end. I had to be back at work in Seoul the following day, and I had set out with the food Mother had prepared for my train ride. I had almost reached the road, the one that was visible from the lakeshore, when I heard the soft crunch of bicycle tires on the dirt path, a sound almost like whispering. It was Ajaebi with his whitening hair. He didn't call out my name, just smiled a toothy, wrinkled smile—a smile whose depth I didn't appreciate until later. The crunch of the tires stopped and he got off the bicycle. There was a shabby basket on the carrying rack, and in it a vase of rose moss.

"Put that on your windowsill and you'll have something to remember me by."

He wheeled the bicycle around, and the crunch of the tires faded into the distance. That was the last time I saw him. I was tied down to my job, and one day during my lengthening absence from home he very suddenly passed away. Leaving me with an aching heart and a vase of rose moss.

My child, why am I so thirsty today, and why is your sleep so deep? All around me is stillness. Wake up, my child, wake up and listen to my words. What if I blink and then see that the lake has come back to life? . . . What if the wheels of the dusty bicycle resting in the shade should start whirling soundlessly by themselves? . . . What if all the whispering in the world should turn into flowing water? . . . My child, I have so much to whisper to you, like I did when you and I were one body. How should I tell the story now? Shall I tell a story of tears, a story of laughter? A story of days gone by, a story of days to come? A story of air, a story of fluid? My child, the sun is still so very hot. . . . Shall I tell you the story like I did when you and I were one body?

Translation by Kichung Kim and Bruce Fulton

The Thirteen-Scent Flower

The Thirteen-Scent Flower

1. North Pole Calling

A late-winter day the year he turned twenty.

His schooling in the ancestral home behind him, he had come to Seoul and worked at a variety of jobs, drumming up business for a dealer in Chindo dogs whom he had met in his peregrinations along the thoroughfare of Chongno and at regular intervals helping out at a moving company. These jobs he worked in order to live were made possible by his ability to drive, a skill he had picked up for the most part by following his uncle around. For what it was worth—and this hopeless period did not last very long—these jobs allowed him to stand on his own two feet.

This uncle, his senior by six years, had left the ancestral home and the few of his relatives who still lived there, establishing himself early on in the big city; he had been forever concerned about his nephew's future, and then one day had suddenly died. Whereupon the uncle's small truck had passed down to the nephew. It had been Uncle's dream to be a pilot, and from his early teens he had worked as an auto mechanic, finally going into business on his own as a truck driver. He liked to putter around with junked-car parts—as if this would help realize his dream—but it needs no explaining that fixing up old cars and learning to pilot aircraft are two starkly different enterprises.

Uncle's dream was not to be just any old pilot but a *fighter* pilot. But he had never earned enough money to take flight lessons. And even if he had, never in his adult life had there been a war that would have allowed him the opportunity to pilot a jet fighter. And so his dream had become worn and tired. Poor Uncle.

It was Uncle who had put him through high school and who, in hopes that his nephew, if not he himself, might someday pilot a light-speed jet fighter, had given unsparingly of the meager earnings for which he had worked himself to the bone. Every time Uncle completed one of the strange contrivances he assembled from auto parts, he would show it to him. Most of these were playthings more than practical mechanisms.

"When I say 'pilot,'" Uncle had said, using the English word, "I don't mean the Pilot brand of fountain pen."

Uncle's lack of any opportunity to realize his overly ambitious dream had made him feel inferior, and his inferiority complex had in turn led him to add "I mean" or "I don't mean" to practically everything he said. He had never been able to rid himself of that habit. And now Uncle was gone for good.

He himself was educated enough to be able to read newspapers, so when Uncle had one of his grieving spells he was able to offer an explanation such as the following: "Uncle, if you really want to be a fighter pilot, you have to be born in the right country. Take the United States. Look at all the wars they've been through—domestic wars and foreign wars. Someone in a country like *that* can be a fighter pilot, easy."

Uncle had had the foresight to prepare a will bequeathing all of his effects to his nephew, on one condition—that his nephew not bury him. And so he had had Uncle cremated, scattering his ashes along the stream in the ancestral village. And this was how he had come to inherit Uncle's truck and all of Uncle's various odds and ends. The majority of these were items of everyday use, nearing the end of their life span, but there were also numerous maps, half a dozen pairs of binoculars, and a dozen or so compasses. He wasn't sure what the latter items had to do with Uncle's dream, but he kept every last one of them, treated them with care, and always took the least used of them when he went out in the truck. The routes he drove, though, were not so complicated as to require the aid of a compass, so he never really had to use it. But on the odd occasions when he drove a quiet byway, he liked to stop, produce the compass, and take a bearing.

"Hmm, north by northwest."

And sometimes the knowledge that he was heading north by northwest was a source of great comfort.

His decision to work as a truck driver for the time being was partly a matter of his inability to think of another way to make a living, but it was also a gesture of respect for Uncle, who had spent a significant portion of his life driving a truck.

His dream, though, was to be a denizen of the Arctic. For a time he rented a room on the outskirts of Seoul, in the home of a man he had met in his comings and goings on Chongno. He signed up for work at a delivery company, driving his truck into Seoul when he was called for a job but otherwise doing repairs or fixing up his landlord's run-down house. He had steady work with the delivery company, and not once did Uncle's truck break down as he drove it around.

During the evening hours he would stare absently at a secondhand television that received only two channels, and he would listen to a handful of tapes of popular songs, or sing along with them, on Uncle's old stereo system, which required a gentle kick to set it in motion. In between these activities he might also gaze at the parts of the ancient mechanical devices Uncle had left him.

Around this time his insomnia had worsened, and when late in the evening his thoughts roamed so far and wide that they interfered with sleep, he sometimes took the truck out onto the expressway. There he entertained notions of making it possible for people who were physically distant from one another to enjoy a deep conversation simply by communicating mind to mind. And there had to be a way to make a ballpoint pen that would automatically record your thoughts if you stuck it over your ear like a carpenter did his pencil. He held especially high hopes for the pen. To explain its uses to the world, he would travel far and wide, expressing himself freely even to those who spoke different tongues, and to those who gathered around him with exclamations he would offer a humble smile. Often, while thinking such thoughts, he would discover that it was after midnight. He was well aware that these nocturnal thoughts were the meaningless musings of the lonely. Still, they were less cruel than Uncle's dream of becoming a fighter pilot; indeed, they represented his best attempt to ward off infection by that dream.

Another way he spent his time was to call to mind the faces of people whose lives had intersected with his only in passing, or the faces of nameless girls who for a moment in time had quickened his heartbeat. Or there would be desultory thoughts, like a spray of water droplets from a spinning tire, of girls his age from the ancestral town, girls who worked at the beautician's or in the factory or in the grocery store. Faces and thoughts that surfaced in the absence of any others.

And so it was that on a frigid winter morning he had set out for downtown in his freshly ironed suit—it was a black one, he had no other—with a red muffler coiled around his neck. He felt like the wretched turkey he had once seen at the zoo, its unremarkable tail spread haughtily wide. Like someone hoping for a miracle or attending to a crucial business matter, he scurried about the city center for the entire day, hands clenched tight in his pockets. You would have thought that had his feet stopped for even an instant, any miraculous opportunity he might have come across would disappear for all time. But when evening finally arrived, not a single miraculous instance had arisen—no person, nothing sufficient to bring cessation to the unutterable loneliness he felt. He observed the young people striding along the cold streets, their energetic smiles. Even their breath visible in the chill air seemed to exude sweetness. They looked no more than twenty, the same as him, yet how could they possibly be the same age?

Enough was enough, and he returned home. Folding his quilt and leaning back against it, he indulged himself in his one and only luxury—beer—and selected one of the maps Uncle had left him, a map of the world. He mounted it on the wall.

And thus began his dreams of the Arctic. When he had nothing better to do he would remove this map from the wall and say out loud the difficult-to-pronounce place names— Ulan Bator, Vladivostok, Sierra Nevada. But the place where his thoughts always came to rest was the Arctic. Ellesmere, Etah, Thule, Reykjavik—he imagined himself traversing Arctic islands, vast snowfields, finally coming upon a tiny settlement. In this way he gradually penetrated the frozen wastes.

Every night he walked the Arctic expanse by himself, the tiny lights of dwellings clustered in the ice retreating before him. The lights seemed to be shining in the distance, and then when he approached they would recede. "If those lights off in the distance don't start getting closer right now, I'm going to end up sprawled out on this ice field." Panting, chilled to the bone, he would mumble this to himself as he put one frozen foot in front of the other and willed himself not to collapse.

One of these nights he would meet a good-hearted Eskimo woman and settle down with her. They would have a nice, dependable reindeer and, to transport their foodstuffs, a team of huskies, and in time they would have children. And when the children were old enough they'd go out on the tundra with him to hunt. His progress through the Arctic snowfields was arduous; he would collapse on the ice, and just before he sank into a final sleep he would awaken.

He wondered, should he actually go to the Arctic? Was the Arctic really a necessary part of this modest dream of his? He would ask himself such questions when he awakened at night to scratch the soles of his feet, feeling as if he actually had gone there and gotten his extremities frostbitten. And the very instant he fell back asleep, there it was again, the Arctic falling away from him for hundreds of miles in all directions, a place without sound, gravity, pain, or sorrow.

And then one night during this period of Arctic trekking, the phone rang from across the flat expanse. It had to be a wrong number, this ringing from the Arctic's frozen wastes, and so he kept moving forward. "Hmm, the air's so nice, it's so still and quiet, the Ice Age must have been like this," he mumbled. And then on the icy plain there appeared a dwelling. He went inside, and that's where the phone was ringing.

He picked up the receiver; it was cold to the touch. Loud static at the other end—strange. And then a faint sigh, as if from right up close. In the languid flow of Arctic time, five minutes must have passed. And then the line went dead.

On the following day, and the day after that, with nightfall came the phone call. When he answered, a voice said hello—always the same voice—and then there was silence. The Arctic woman wouldn't speak unless he spoke first. If he didn't speak for a while, she didn't either.

Meanwhile, he continued to work. People were forever on the move in this city, leaving one home and moving to another, countless people, and there were stretches when every morning without fail he was called on, and so he crisscrossed the city, sometimes to transport dozens of oil drums, sometimes to move a beat-up wardrobe and a pedal sewing machine, or maybe to help with the belongings of a woman who had been sent packing from her home. But there were also days when he arrived at the assigned place to find that the people had canceled at the last minute, and there were days when he wasn't called at all.

And still he knew nothing about the Arctic apart from a few photos and—long before, something he remembered only faintly—a television program about a day in the life of an Eskimo man and wife. At night he still talked to himself about the Arctic before falling asleep.

He dreamed he was a young Eskimo man named Byehagit'u. He was on his way home from a journey so long he couldn't remember when he had departed. He had wanted to return with much meat and many skins, but the winter ice had crushed his raft and the only thing he had managed to save—and that barely—was himself. He had survived the winter blizzards with a family of seals, had assisted in the birth of a pup on a bed hollowed out of thick ice by the mother,

her teeth visible among icicle-festooned whiskers. In the meantime, many changes had taken place in the Arctic. Sixteen at the time he had left his family's igloo, he was now a fully grown man. Compass in hand, he walked and he walked in the direction of home, but his settlement did not appear. He walked ceaselessly across the dark ice fields, for if he stopped he would freeze and die. And on one white night when he could no longer remember how long he had walked, he came across a lone Eskimo woman hauling a funny-looking beat-up sled. . . .

2. Green Hands

Gonna run out in front of the next car that comes along. It was late at night and she was concealed by the blackness of the woods that shaded the highway. Once she'd made up her mind, she had walked hours to get here, found a bend in the road that suited her purposes, and hunkered down inside a stand of bushy young pines. She had crawled through the brush to reach this curve, the branches of the pines tickling her cheeks and making her giggle, the forlorn lights along the highway filtering faintly through the growth.

She had already watched several vehicles pass by. *Not gonna jump in front of just any old car*, she muttered again as she shivered in the chill air of early spring. Talking to herself like this served to steel her ever-flagging physical energies. From where she sat, the lights of oncoming cars could be seen in the distance. The bend in the highway curved toward her so that she would have ample time, when finally she decided, to run out in front of her chosen vehicle.

She wasn't counting the number of vehicles she had watched pass by since she'd crouched down in this spot. She was more concerned about the illusion she had of being pushed back over a nonexistent outcrop behind her. *I'm not afraid*, she had told herself countless times during the hours it had taken her to walk here. A shadow sprang from the gloom. She jumped up, saw it was only a feral cat, but at the same time stumbled and fell forward. This trifling incident gave her a fresh taste of fear.

Not gonna jump in front of just any old car! She bit down hard on her lip. That lower lip was unusually plump and fleshy, owing to the many sorrows she had experienced as a child, causing her frequently to pout and bite down. The cold air made its way beside her, and with a faint shiver she began to sing a song from her childhood while she awaited just the right car.

Her ancestral home was about as remote as you can get in the mountains. She had no siblings and her parents were no longer alive. When she had opened her eyes to the world for the first time there was only her grandmother, by then so old she appeared to be more than a hundred. There was much she just couldn't understand—how she had come to be born in the first place, how she had spent her first twelve years tucked away high up in the mountains, how she had moved from her hillside town to the small city, and from the small city to the big city, and how at every turn she had met with bad luck. Nor did she know why she had been sent packing from every place she had ever worked, finally to find herself on the road back to her ancestral home.

So many things had happened to her, too many to find space in her still-developing brain. She imagined the inside of her head consisting of small containers that were just the right size but slightly the worse for wear, kind of like the paper box of cookies with the picture on it that a distant relative had left her grandmother after a visit to the home deep in the mountains, small containers full of items from around and about home—bits of string, dried leaves, and shards of stone—on which the covers never fit tight and that were worn at the creases. There were keys to unlock these containers in her mind, but she could never remember where they were.

What she did remember was the whirlwind that had swept her up the moment she made the decision to throw herself in front of a car, a spur-of-the-moment decision she had made on the bus back to Grandmother and the ancestral home. And yet she couldn't have explained what was compelling her to take her own life. She was sixteen years of age—sixteen. Death to this sixteen-year-old girl was something easy to carry out, something sweet, a nymph hovering, offering to solve her difficulties. For some time she had carried on a conversation with this honey-voiced nymph, starting the day she was sent packing, for the flimsiest reason, from a home where she had looked after the daughter, steamed the rice, and cooked the stew. But she couldn't say it was due to these conversations that she would kill herself. It was obvious that everybody held her in contempt—they always did. Everybody? But that didn't really make sense, because she didn't know that many people. *But nobody's gonna ask me anyway. By the time they do, I'll already be dead. And dead people can't answer.*

The last several years seemed to have been always winter, an early morning mountain landscape of desolation and sorrow. Such was the life of this sixteen-year-old girl who used to pass the days singing songs like this one that she'd learned from the landlord's daughter:

Cukes in the cuke patch, nice and slim
Nice and slim here, nice and slim there,
Says roly-poly squash, come for a visit:
Boo hoo hoo, I'm fat!

Peppers in the pepper patch, sharp and pointy
Sharp and pointy here, sharp and pointy there,
Says nice round apple, come for a visit:
Ow ow ow, that smarts!

It was through no mistake of hers that this girl she looked after had died, yet she was beaten by the landlord and sent packing the same night. All she was able to take with her was a pot of gardenias she had kept on the tiny balcony. The landlady had claimed that there was something peculiar about the water she gave those gardenias, which in turn produced a scent that was too strong, and that this was why their daughter had died. In fact the daughter, a tiny four-year-old girl, had had a heart ailment. She knew she had been sent away because the girl's young parents were in such pain from having lost her.

She proceeded from one family to the next. But from each and every house she was sent packing, and never for a reason she could understand. At one house the landlord's son forced his way into her room; at another the landlord got drunk and beat her. Ultimately the pot of gardenias died, and after some time she found herself working at a nursery. This first job at a nursery was a period that overflowed with laughter. That is, until she was sent away for liberating the saplings—the big-cone and other pines, the maples, and the boxwoods—from the wire that kept them dwarfed, and then watering them to their hearts' content. From there the pattern continued—find employment at a nursery and before long be sent packing.

A vehicle passed by, a mid-size truck. *Not that one*, she muttered with a slight shake of her head. It bustled along stupidly, headlights glaring like the bloodshot eyes of a drunken bum, before speeding past the brush where she crouched. There was a whoosh all about her and the highway fell silent once again.

Gonna get squashed, crushed, flattened. Through the sleeves of her worn coat she felt for her fleshy arms. And then her hands, the thick rough hands that her grandmother had called "green hands." Green hands because they did such a good job of producing crops from slash-and-burn fields and stony ground alike. A gatherer of medicinal herbs who had obtained lodging for the night from her grandmother, slack-jawed in amazement that the girl had located deep within the mountains a place where such herbs grew, taking his cue from her grandmother and the other villagers, called the girl Green Hands in recognition of her talent. And that's what she was called at the first of the nurseries where she worked, a nursery in town where she had gone at the recommendation of the herb gatherer. It was only in the city that she wasn't called Green Hands. At the flower shop where she had worked, they had given her the name Miss O—supposedly it was easier for the customers that way. And so at this point there was no one who called her Green Hands.

She passed her hands over her breasts, which had developed a faint ache. She wanted to kill herself before those breasts could take visible shape. If this was part of growing up, then she wanted nothing to do with it. Not once since she left home had she felt that her body was developing as it should, nice and normally. But now as she crouched in the dark there was a firm elasticity to her flesh, a sensation both full and immediate. And this surprised her. She thought about how all of it would be *squashed, crushed, flattened* beneath the wheels of a car, and tears began to dribble from her eyes. She could almost hear the voices: *Green Hands! Where are you?* Her grandmother's voice would be in there somewhere, and the voices of other people back home. She wiped away her tears and listened. But there was only the soughing of the wind coming down from the hills to tickle the ground before moving on.

There, a vehicle on the way, its arrival announced by the white upward slant of its brights. She stirred and the car came into view, motoring shyly along, a compact whose small size was out of all proportion to the beams of light it cast. And at that very moment hot tears gushed forth and streamed down her cheeks, unleashed by the memory of her grandmother's appearance that day she had stolen unnoticed from home before dawn.

Was her grandmother still alive? Or was she dead by now? And how about the handful of other villagers who lived at the foot of the mountain—were they still there, or had they left too? Her small grandmother had been curled up asleep. No way she would know that the girl was leaving. The next morning, like all the others, Grandmother would have had her fetch water upon rising, turned her out to the fields, had lunch with her. . . . As the distance between her and the ancestral village grew and grew and she turned back for a momentary look, she realized that the mountain peaks all around her were no longer the peaks she had been accustomed to seeing. The swift play of her moving feet came to a stop and she plopped herself down. She was on a mountain road, just outside a small village. She undid the ties of her cloth bag, intending to eat one of the rice balls she had packed, and there inside the cloth bundle of her belongings were mugwort rice cakes and money. Grandmother had known after all, even though the girl had been hiding the bag among the farm tools lying neglected beneath the veranda. . . .

Added to her exhaustion, the surge of all these memories was too much for her—she fell asleep. She fell deep and far, not into a momentary doze but into a dream in which she fought to extricate herself from the clutches of creatures who predated her existence on earth, dinosaurs and such, reptiles whose names she didn't know. She was awakened by her own hacking cough, the shaking of her head, and at that very moment she saw a vehicle with a single funny-looking headlight creaking toward her. It was so funny-looking that her frightening dream of a moment before was forgotten.

That's the one! she murmured as she rubbed her eyes awake. The light from this one-eyed vehicle seemed to be mounted higher than on normal cars, and when it rounded the bend in the highway she saw why—it was a little truck. She had just readied herself to run out to the roadside, was just about to rise to her feet when the truck coughed and wheezed and sputtered to a stop nearby.

A man got out, holding a flashlight, and made a circuit of the truck, giving each of the tires a little kick. Her gaze followed the play of light on the porcupinelike truck; it was almost as if the flashlight were meant to light her way. At the same time, the frightful pulsation of her heart, quickened by expectations of the death for which she had readied herself, began slowly to ease. *What now?* There were the wheels, right in front of her, the wheels she had to throw herself under, and they'd stopped—just stopped!

He was a shriveled little guy, and young. It was all she could do to avoid calling out "Hello there!" He was slightly bent over, legs apart, and from the rear, flashlight in hand, he struck her as different from all the countless men she had happened till now to see from the rear. She was reminded of a story she had heard back home, about how when fog formed along Foggy Peak in the winter, all the cares of this world were gathered up and then spirited away. Whenever the winds of winter drove up against Foggy Peak, a column of fog would form, taking the shape of a man—so this story went. And now she was afraid that the man standing with his back to her would turn into fog and drift away.

Vehicles passed by the stationary truck. She remained where she was, sitting on her bag with its cloth bundle. Finally she rose. Hearing the man whistle a tune and seeing him look off into the distance below, where the lights of the city were visible, she crept into the truck on the passenger side. When the man returned to his truck he discovered a woman he had never seen before. He was surprised enough to have asked her detailed questions, but instead he merely, and only briefly, considered her mottled, unwashed face, the shabby bag, and her muddy feet. The truck sputtered to life and away they went. She took one last look back toward the city she had just left.

In the wee hours of the following morning, in an area on the outskirts of the city where the nurseries were lined up one after another, she got out of the truck and waited for dawn. And it being spring, with helping hands in demand, she found work at one of the nurseries. There for the first time she introduced herself as Green Hands. She wasn't paid a wage, but was given a place to sleep in return for changing the soil in several hundred flowerpots. This time she refrained from undoing the wire that was wound tight around the little pines and maples. And no more did she walk along the highway intending to throw herself beneath the wheels of a speeding car.

She had a difficult time sleeping through the night. Exhaustion would cause her to doze off early in the evening, however, and at such times she dreamed she had turned into a whimpering little fir tree. Before, dozing often gave rise to a dream in which she fell off a cliff. "Girls and boys who are growing up have such dreams," her grandmother would tell her. Now that she had grown as much as she ever would, she no longer believed this. And now, at the nursery, she had another dream of tumbling over a cliff, and when she awakened she thought of the old one-eyed truck she had come across on that hair-raising night along the highway. And she thought of the man who from the rear resembled a column of fog.

Still clear in her mind was the word "Mover" and the telephone number painted on the side of the truck, illuminated by the flashlight that night. The numbers now blinked on in her mind, each a different color and all of them winking like little holiday lights. She called that number. And at first she said nothing, listening to the voice of the man at the other end. Every evening. The evening haze would settle near the nursery and when the hour grew late, the urge to throw herself under a speeding car on the highway would seethe and take hold of her, and that's when she called. Every evening, every single evening.

3. *The Advent of the Wind Chrysanthemum*

It was on a bright sunny day that Bye and Green Hands met for the first time since Bye had dropped her off at the nurseries. They met at a clearing on the hill behind the nursery where Green Hands worked. It was so sunny that from this hill they could see heat shimmers, which normally didn't appear till later in the season. Some ten feet from where they stood was a budding rosebay, but they were not yet comfortable enough together to appreciate it—it was all they could do to get the words of introduction out of their mouths.

"You can call me Bye. I made that name myself. By day I move things for people and by night I dream about going to the Arctic. 'Bye' means a man who walks the Arctic flats."

"My name is Green Hands. I was born in a village up in the mountains. I'll be seventeen in September."

They hadn't realized, in the dim light of the trucks passing on the highway that first night, what they now knew from each other's face—that from an infinite distance in the distant past they had gradually been approaching each other. They had been alone for so long that for the moment they could say nothing beyond this initial exchange, could only glare at each other as if something had angered them. They were as silent as the woman from the Arctic who called each night, the woman who didn't speak unless spoken to. The man who received the call each night, who had been whistling beside the highway, set Green Hands' hands atremble more than she had ever thought possible, creating in her a heart-dropping sensation of oppression that left her wishing she could have run away right then and there. Far from running away, though, neither of them could manage a word to the other, for they had both come down with a fever, a symptom of a peculiar infectious disease.

The precursor of this fever was a feeling of sadness. To Bye, Green Hands looked sad, and to Green Hands, Bye looked sad. Each saw, reflected in the innocent eyes of the other, eyes that were sad—sad because each knew not what to do—and the realization that this was what it was like for two people to meet for the first time was in itself sad. This sadness, though, was nothing compared with the onslaught of the fever that night.

Back at their respective lodgings Bye covered himself with his quilt while Green Hands lay down in her bedding at the nursery, head cradled in her arm, and all through that night each of them engaged in a delirious struggle with the fever that baked them. They were in the throes of a disease, but which disease—typhoid fever, dysentery, measles, cholera?— they didn't know. All through the night perspiration streamed from their faces. The following morning their fever had

eased, but looking in the moonlike sliver of a mirror that
hung from Bye's faucet, and looking in the half-moon mirror
hanging like a captured bird with bound wings from a post in
Green Hands' nursery, they realized how sunken were their
cheeks and how feverish the gleam in their eyes. In Bye's case
the eyes that gave many people a peculiar impression had developed dark shadows, and in the case of Green Hands her
dimples had deepened overnight so that she seemed always to
be laughing, even when she wasn't—though Green Hands, in
the grip of this mortal fever that had swept over her like a
millennial tidal wave, was scarcely in a position to laugh.

And so ended that long and lonely first night. But that was
not the end of the strange goings-on that befell them. Early
the next morning, directions in hand, Bye set out in his truck
to transport a piano from the southwestern to the northeast-
ern part of the city, a pianist with a melancholy voice having
called a week earlier to schedule the move. But before Bye
knew it the truck had turned down an unfamiliar street and
was accelerating furiously. The faint bluish mist of morning
was dissipating, and with the truck's every lurch and skid,
Bye thought he could hear a martial tune coming from the
piano. Bye was beginning to lose track of the time when the
truck came to an abrupt stop in front of the nursery where Green
Hands worked. No one was more surprised at this than Bye
himself.

At this hour Green Hands was already at work inside one
of the greenhouses, intending to fill her small watering pot to
water a Kaffir lily she had just repotted to make it grow
straight—its owner had arranged to pick it up that day. But
her steps kept taking her in the direction of the doorway,
which was partly covered with a sheet of vinyl, and her hands
hastened to move a tall quintuple bush that was blocking the
entrance. She flung open the plastic covering and whom did

she see standing there but Bye, his face haggard and his eyes sunken. She gave a faint gasp of surprise.

And that was how it went, this first week they knew each other. They would discover themselves standing mutely opposite each other not knowing what had brought them together, or how or when they had arrived there. It was as if sheets of torrential rain had washed them up together. They would observe each other for the longest time, Bye and Green Hands, as if their eyes were magnets. And it wasn't just their eyes that seemed to attract in this way; a magnetic power emanated as well from their extremities, so that their feet, hands, heads, and chests, once they were in close enough proximity, would suddenly collide.

This magnetism infused their lips as well, one time bringing their mouths together with such force that Green Hands was afraid she had broken a tooth. It was the magnetism of their lips that they liked best of all—through various manifestations they had come to feel that among the various parts of their bodies it was their magnetic lips that worked most powerfully. They felt as if they had been sucked into a long tunnel lit by countless red lamps and were slowly dissipating into a dome of air that was a blinding, mountaintop blue and breathtakingly clear. The sensation reminded Green Hands of the mountaintops back home, and Bye of the Arctic of his dreams.

"Green Hands, you look surprised."

"Just now I could see the tops of the mountains back home. I thought I had forgotten them."

"Well, I've been walking across the Arctic flats."

"What's there, on those flats?"

"There was you, and there were snowfields."

"You were there, Bye, on the mountaintops back home. And those mountaintops were always covered with snow."

In the meantime an objection was made to the owner of the nursery by a customer who was somehow delivered an orange tree instead of a gardenia, and a runaway girl's travel bag was delivered to the bedroom of a single man. There were complaints from the customers, but there was also the occasional customer who was enchanted by a Benjamin bush that was twice as leafy as normal, or bewitched by the odd sight of a *yang* orchid with seven stamens crowned with white petals. And a little old withered sickle orchid that hadn't bloomed in years suddenly sprouted three blossoms. By now the owner was utterly confounded: what was he to do with Green Hands? If it were up to her, she would have spent every spare moment up the hill behind the nursery seeing Bye. And if it were up to the owner, he would have sent her packing as soon as she came down from the hill, but whenever he summoned her and she appeared before him, he somehow lost courage.

The magnetism between Bye and Green Hands had grown ever stronger and more active, until they couldn't be apart for a moment. They longed for each other with such a passion that it made them depressed. Even when they were face to face, Bye's head felt heavy and clouded the whole day long, as if he were running nonstop day and night along an indistinct path in a land of constant night; while Green Hands had the dizzying sensation of sinking ever deeper into a bottomless well, as if she were a pebble dropped into the water by a thirsty boy. It was worse now than before they had met, harder on them than the lonely dreams that had visited Bye and the gloomy fancies that had drifted through Green Hands' mind as she walked alone along the highway. If only they could, they would have penetrated each other's bones, fusing themselves into one. They wanted to consume each other. And that craving paralyzed them. For they were too young to comprehend the phenomenon of desire in all its capriciousness.

Bye had no mind to be doing his moving work, and Green Hands could no longer abide the sight of the white sap leaking out of the verdant flesh of the dwarf trees where they were bound by the wire that stunted their growth.

One late-spring day they were lying on a hill watching the lazy shapes formed by the yellowish clouds. Green Hands broke the silence:

"Bye, how far could the truck go on a full tank of gas?"

"Very very far, Green Hands, very very far."

They had come to the same conclusion: they would go off somewhere. And for the very first time since they had met, they spent the day apart—each preparing for departure.

"Think like we're going to a deserted island, and taking only what's absolutely essential."

"That's right, only what's absolutely essential."

For Green Hands there was nothing to take besides a few garments. She could be ready to leave in no time. Her clothing, such as it was, was old and worn, but because the pockets all contained seeds—when and why she had put them there, she didn't know—she couldn't very well throw those clothes away. Making sure the seeds didn't spill out, she carefully folded and packed them in a small bag. Nothing to do now but sit and wait for Bye.

As she often did when alone, she laughed to herself. For she had thought up a way to wait for Bye without getting bored. The nursery had a window with an awning, and in front of it three rows of saplings. She began to undo the wire that bound them. In one place the wire had cut so deeply into the wood that she had to take a pair of wire cutters to it. After she had freed every one of those dozens of trees she filled a huge watering can and gave them all a good sprinkling. Experience had taught her that she had only to look at the sky to tell when she should water the saplings and how much. And now she looked at the sky intending to water the pots that the owner always stuck in the shade and left untended. In that sky, night was approaching from afar.

Meanwhile Bye was out in the backyard sorting through the rusted implements in the huge box containing the inheritance from his uncle. Items such as map and compass he put in the truck. These amounted to a small pile. With every item he added to the truck he asked himself: Would this be absolutely essential on a desert island? The last thing he did was go inside to bid farewell to his landlord, who had been kind to him as no one else had. The packing had taken only a short time, but the farewells to the landlord and his family ended up taking almost the entire day.

When the landlord's family heard what Bye and Green Hands intended to do, they held a spirited exchange of views about which items were essential if one was starting a new life. When at the end of a very long debate they couldn't come to a conclusion, they decided that the least they could do was, each of them, think of one item that was absolutely essential, and these they placed in the truck as a gift. And so besides what Bye had packed there were in the truck a huge bottle of spirits that the landlord had kept deep inside a closet, a rice pot from the landlady, bedding from the elder daughter, a silk necktie from the elder son, and a week-old puppy from the younger son.

It was late at night by the time Bye and Green Hands were able to leave. Bye produced the compass and they set out in a southerly direction. A week later they were heading northwest; a month later they were heading northeast. They drove in every direction, worrying not about the time, their next meal, or where they would spend the night. To overcome the incomprehensible loneliness that had taken hold of them, they did the one sole thing they could, and that was to drive the truck forward, ever forward, night and day. There were days when they drove until the faint light of dawn peeked over the dark ridgeline of the mountains. At such times they stopped the truck, held each other tight, and gazed silently at the first light. Their destination was a desert island, wherever that might be. From time to time they would spend a few days working at a restaurant, a construction site, or a farm, earning enough to subsist, and after several months of driving along like this they found themselves at Green Hands' ancestral home.

Time passed, and in the year that Bye turned twenty-two and Green Hands nineteen they witnessed the advent of a rare flower. They named it the wind chrysanthemum.

4. The Secret of the Wind Chrysanthemum

Is there anyone who can speak with certainty about the wind chrysanthemum—about its appearance, its scent, about the untold story of its advent?

> Wind chrysanthemum. Commonly known as the Arctic Flower. Hardy plant living in a land of bitter cold, your tender blossoms streaming in winter's north wind beneath high clouds; your delicate purple blossoms reaching out for the sunlight shining through the clouds, symbol of your thirst for life; your fifty-five petals ever mindful that your beauty is based on the number five; your snow-white scent a distillate of the manifold desires embodied in your small form, a sad dedication to the world. You are short of stature, the better to confront the arid climate; your lonely leaves are green year round; your humble stems are protected by fine wool.

This example of "flower writing" is one of the few surviving texts concerning the wind chrysanthemum.

Neither Bye nor Green Hands could have explained how they managed to create a habitat for their unusual flower. To be sure, they still remembered vividly the day they discovered the wind chrysanthemum. It would have been difficult for them to predict, though, that this flower, a few withered specimens of which they saw that first night, would later excite people to the extent it did. Who would have believed that Bye would provide it with a diet of Arctic wind, or that Green Hands would stay up a thousand nights to watch over it? Only afterward did one and all begin to call this flower the wind chrysanthemum.

When Bye and Green Hands had arrived at her ancestral home, a mountain village that enjoyed minimal sunshine, they found that the villagers had moved away, so it was in effect unpopulated. As they looked out from a mountaintop at the desolation, the happiest of all was their puppy, Tchangi, who had thwarted death several times in the course of their long journey in the truck. In her house on the ridge with its view down the ridgeline, Green Hands' grandmother had awaited the homecoming of her granddaughter so that she might close her eyes in peace. With their arrival she was finally able to do just that, and so the first thing Bye did was dig a small grave in which to lay the elderly woman's shriveled form.

"I have lived a long life, and you may now say good-bye to me forever. Beside my grave sprinkle seeds from the bag beneath the veranda."

Such were Grandmother's last words. Green Hands found the brown bag, which she had known ever since she was a child, added to its seeds those scattered among her pockets, and sprinkled them all together around her grandmother's grave. Because it was late autumn, Green Hands' heart ached even while she sprinkled the seeds to relieve the sorrow of her grandmother's passing. For she knew those seeds would not sprout.

Having buried Grandmother and readied themselves for winter, Bye and Green Hands were able to sleep soundly for the first time since they had met, putting out of their minds their loneliness, their hunger, the cold, and their unease. So short were the days this deep and high in the mountains that they sometimes awoke to surroundings gloomy as night, and went right back to sleep. And there were times when they were afraid to open their eyes and slept on instead. One winter day, when they had awakened from one such lengthy night of sleep, they saw up behind the house five flowers the color of light maroon, a plant that seemed to have forgotten the season in which it was supposed to bloom.

Green Hands was the first to see this flowering plant. She had gone outside to a night of fist-sized snowflakes, and she felt as if her breath would crystallize into thick clouds. Flashlight in hand, braving the bitter north wind, she could imagine her grandmother declaring that this was the worst cold in her eighty-seven years. It was too late now to bring the flowers inside, and so certain was Green Hands that they would not survive that she thought she would say good-bye to them. But what she saw made her cry out in surprise. In the swirling snow, which made breathing difficult, buffeted by the wind, an angelic soprano voice coming over the ridge, she saw it plainly in the dim light of her flashlight: those five light maroon flowers were actually stretching out into the wind—they were blossoming!

Carefully she removed the clear plastic covering from the plants. In the harsh wind, which threatened to rip the delicate petals asunder at any moment, the flowers had clearly been growing, their stalks standing up like the ears of an owl that has heard a mysterious sound. Seeing that they resembled chrysanthemums, these flowers blossoming miraculously in the wind, Green Hands christened them wind chrysanthemums.

Bye's reaction, when he came outside in response to Green Hands' outcry, was different: "I've seen those flowers somewhere." As he watched the buds slowly open to reveal the petals inside, he thought he had seen them in a picture, and that they might be the one and only plant that blooms in the Arctic. But for Green Hands, who had seen countless flowers in her childhood home here at Land's End, where alpine flowers flourished, such a plant as this was new.

They dug the flowers out of the ground, and before long the winds had died down and sunshine was pouring over the mountaintops. But from that point on, the plants began a long decline. The petals grew feeble, the stalks thin; one of the five flowers began to droop, and on a warm clear day it died. They watered the flowers, provided them with a nice warm plastic covering, potted them, and brought them inside, but nothing helped. Green Hands was bothered endlessly by the death of the one flower, until she saw that the remaining four went through the same life cycle, blooming and then dying.

How long would it take them to make a small habitat in which they could revive the withering wind chrysanthemums? A long time, as it turned out. Bye and Green Hands familiarized themselves with the physiology of the plant, engendered ten flowers from the original five, and eventually made a plot of wind chrysanthemums that covered the area below the ridge. During this long process they learned that the wind chrysanthemum preferred to sink its roots in ground that was cold and shaded, that it didn't like rainwater or dew that hadn't been filtered first, that its light maroon color deepened slightly in winter, that its scent was stronger when the cold wind blew. And they realized after long observation that the white wool that covered the stalks secreted a thin white sap that could hardly be seen by the naked eye.

Each of the wind chrysanthemums had a slightly different scent, which was strongest at dawn and late at night, and frequent were the times that Bye and Green Hands slept poorly because of these fragrances. On such nights they might find themselves, eyes wide open, flying on the back of a huge white creature over a turquoise land of mystery or navigating among phosphorescent rocks in the deep blue sea.

To provide the conditions necessary for the wind chrysanthemum to bloom—the cold, the heavy snow, the strong wind—Bye fashioned from his uncle's inheritance an apparatus that used a propeller to create a strong Arctic wind. All of his passion went into this project. Years of experience taught Bye and Green Hands that the wind chrysanthemum was at its strongest, produced its deepest scent, and blossomed for the longest time when baptized with thirty-three days of strong wind and heavy snow.

To induce a stronger scent from the flowers, Green Hands tried new regimens: in spring water from the mountaintops she mixed gardenia sap, hotroot, and smoky hemp; on the seventh day of the seventh lunar month, All Souls Day, she collected rainwater, let it sit for fifty-five days, then added to it a combination of new bush-clover shoots, angelica root, and bunting feathers. Watering the wind chrysanthemums with these different mixtures made their scents delicately different. Time passed and Green Hands' loneliness was lost to oblivion.

Afterward, when people flocked to the mountain village to ask the secret of the wind chrysanthemum's scent, Green

Hands was unable to answer. The people then attacked her, as dilettantes sometimes do, saying she was afraid to share the wind chrysanthemums and would have them believe that the scent had simply materialized all by itself. But the reason Green Hands couldn't answer was that there were so many different trials involved in improvising the mixtures with which she watered the chrysanthemums. It was those mixtures that made the scents of the various flowers delicately different, and to each of the scents she attached a name. But even if she had had to spend half a day outlining all the ingredients of the various mixtures to those who asked the secret, it would have been no use. For one thing, her recollections were often confused, and because the people were unable to detect the slight difference among the scents, none of them would have believed what she said.

In the nearby town, as elsewhere in the countryside, every fifth day was market day, and on those days Bye and Green Hands found a shady spot to set up business. But their initial attempts to introduce the wind chrysanthemum to the public were futile, for people paid no attention to this perennial plant with the pale-looking light maroon flowers, a plant that grew no more than a hand span in height. Bye and Green Hands had selected ten hardy chrysanthemums, stalks and leaves firm from more than thirty-three days of Arctic wind, and placed them in pots that Bye himself had hollowed out of tree trunks, but when the evening mist had settled and the time approached for the market to close down, they had attracted the gaze of no one except a few children who, drawn instinctually by the mysterious scent, had slipped away from their parents and gathered around the pots. But the parents presently arrived, and after casting suspicious looks at Bye and Green Hands they retrieved their children.

Bye and Green Hands were running critically low on fuel for the propeller that produced the Arctic wind, so they took the ten wind chrysanthemums to the largest nursery in town and offered them at a bargain price. But the owners had never seen such plants before, and taking them for wild chamomiles or weeds that happened to blossom in the fall, they showed not the slightest interest. An opportunity to enchant one of the owners was lost when Green Hands brought one of the chrysanthemums up close to the man's nose, where, to her misfortune, its delicate fragrance was masked by those of other flowers.

Nothing to do but put the ten pots nestling the little wind chrysanthemums back into the truck. They sputtered along a dark road through woods that had sucked up most of the daylight. Heading south-southeast in the direction of Land's End, they stopped briefly in a village of a dozen households—the very same place where Green Hands, after leaving home, had looked back at the ridgeline as she ate the mugwort rice cakes that her grandmother had made for her. The village felt cozy surrounded by the folds of mountains now enveloped in darkness, and it offered infinite solace to their weary minds. Bye could now understand Green Hands' desolate state the day she had left her ancestral home, and it occurred to him that they should leave one of the wind chrysanthemums with each of the families in this village. The weak lights in the houses flickered out and the scent of the wind chrysanthemums was delivered, like a hurried dream, to the windows behind which the weary villagers were proceeding to dreamland.

The villagers woke up the next morning to see these plants that had come seemingly from nowhere. They bloomed for a season, and when they had withered and died the villagers went into the woods to find another such plant and see if it was still blooming. They caught the scent and followed it, making their way gradually uphill, and finally they came upon the small habitat that Bye and Green Hands had created for the wind chrysanthemums. And thus it came about that several of the families in that village moved to Land's End.

In this way the wind chrysanthemum spread to the adjoining village, and to the next village down the mountain, and from there to town, and on to a small city.

Other habitats were created for the wind chrysanthemums and other Arctic wind propellers were erected. Meanwhile Green Hands and Bye had learned that the color of the blossoms differed slightly with the direction and speed of the Arctic wind and with the type of scent, and they wandered the countryside, high and low, trying to find the best way to harmonize the wind chrysanthemum's color and fragrance.

To that point they had cultivated eight different scents. There was Ocean scent, which reminded them of the calm of the ocean deeps; Wind scent, which called to mind the purity of winds sweeping vast plateaus; Deep Blue scent, evoking the primitive ecstasy of a prehistoric paradise; and Fadeaway scent, which revived vague memories buried in the far reaches of time—when they had first smelled each of these, they had given it a name in accordance with the scene that came to mind.

From the next village down the mountain and from the small city nearby, people arrived to settle in Land's End, the birthplace of the wind chrysanthemum, dedicating themselves to propagating the plant far and near. By the time the local village head, responding to a report of a mass movement of people into the area, arrived bearing a warning from the provincial governor, wind chrysanthemums covered half the ridge and dozens of families were scattered in the surrounding area.

5. The Wind Chrysanthemum Craze

People arrived from distant places as well to see the wind chrysanthemum habitat at Land's End. The very first was a breathless man whose pale face seemed to indicate that he had come directly, nonstop, from thousands of miles away. He entered the yard, offered a greeting, then declared, "I am a wind chrysanthemum kind of man."

Bye and Green Hands were puzzled.

"If it wouldn't be too much of a bother, I'd like to study this flower. I hope you will allow me to do so."

The man introduced himself as Ko and said he suffered from low-altitude sickness. Just like the wind chrysanthemum, he needed the cold air and strong winds of a mountain environment to avoid compromising his health. He was barely in his forties, but had learned as a young adult that he had the disease and for almost twenty years had traveled the country's mountainous regions in search of a cure, with little to show for it. And then, during a sojourn in the snowy mountains of a neighboring land, he had learned of the wind chrysanthemum. Bye and Green Hands knew nothing about low-altitude sickness, but when they heard Ko say that he was as worn down, body and soul, as the footwear of the mystics who had been roaming the deserts of the globe for centuries, they welcomed him to Land's End, agreeing to tell him everything he wanted to know about the wind chrysanthemum.

And so Ko fashioned a dugout in between the propeller and the wind chrysanthemums, determined to spend the remainder of his life researching this flower whose health was intertwined with his own. He began to fill his dugout with all manner of experimental apparatus, and every weekend he journeyed to a city six hours distant with test tubes containing his gatherings of the previous week, to work at a friend's laboratory.

"I can't believe I finally found my life's work," he could be heard mumbling. "I never knew a man could be this happy."

Apart from his weekend trips to the city, Ko devoted himself to a solitary life of research until he quite forgot that he suffered from low-altitude sickness, and in two years' time he had developed the Byegreen pill, coining the name from those of Bye and Green Hands as a gesture of gratitude. Even so, he frequently lapsed into despair, longing to discover at least one other person with the same malady. To popularize his Byegreen pill Ko took advantage of every opportunity to advertise in the newspapers for others who suffered from low-altitude sickness, exhausting his assets thereby, while also writing letters to numerous pharmaceutical companies informing them of the results of his research and offering them his pill—never forgetting to place a petal in the envelope so that his stationery would bear the scent of the wind chrysanthemum.

But alas, he received only rejection letters, delivered by a postman who was forever lamenting his miserable lot at having to clamber all the way up a mountain to deliver mail to one person only, and a person who suffered from low-altitude sickness at that! Time passed and even the rejection letters grew scarce, until finally Ko was struck by the thought that he might be the only person in the country with low-altitude sickness. By then the postman's visits had dwindled to a measly once every three or four weeks, and finally they ceased altogether.

Ko's disappointment was so great that Green Hands almost wished she had low-altitude sickness herself, if that would be any consolation. So concerned was she that she picked forty-two of the most fragrant and colorful wind chrysanthemums and wove the stems into a basket, which she then filled with the forty-two dried flowers before presenting this gift to Ko on his forty-second birthday. Ten different scents mingled in this basket, and like the music from an ensemble of instruments with perfect harmony, they spread from Ko's dugout to the village of Land's End, from the village to the mountaintop, and thence to the sky.

The wind chrysanthemum craze began modestly enough, just like the southerly wind of May that the people of Land's End called the *marang*. At first it spread covertly, like the scent of the wind chrysanthemum itself. Not all the scents had the same reach, but a few ranged as far afield as twenty or thirty miles. Whatever their range, people caught the fragrance and came to Land's End to see for themselves where the wind chrysanthemums grew. Poets sang of the scent and color, and at least one bard announced he would compose epic poems recounting the exploits of Bye and Green Hands with their flower. It was around this time that a poem, "Arctic Flower," appeared in the newspaper. At first this lyric, penned by a man named K, drew no special notice, but then it began to pass from mouth to mouth and people started to recite it, until finally a composer who belonged to a nature lovers' club set the words to music, producing a song that everyone sang with delight:

> Long-forgotten mountain village where high clouds come
> to rest
> We pray for eternity in the maidenly wind from the
> Arctic
> You blossomed through the meeting of two lonely souls
> Wind chrysanthemum, so tender yet strong.

In the pale violet of sunset you dream of primeval peace
You are the dreamlike scent of the lover longing for the
 Arctic
Your countless petals, issue of eternal desire
Wind chrysanthemum, essence of eternal beauty.

We offer up our love
We offer up our innocence
May your fragrance numb misfortune
May your brightness diminish sorrow.

The wind chrysanthemum craze, starting so innocuously like the *marang* southerly of May, its direction as uncertain as the *map'a* airflow and its fresh breezes are to the people of Land's End, really took off with the popularity of the "Arctic Flower" song. Numerous people made the steep climb to Land's End. Among them were the inevitable reporters wanting interviews as well as a photographer intent on capturing the wind chrysanthemum for a calendar, who wished first to mount an exhibition of wind chrysanthemum photographs, to which end he brought five cameras and two assistants. Up the trees the photographer and his helpers climbed for shots of the plant's habitat; prone on the ground they lay for close-ups of the flowers.

Also captured in photographs were Bye, standing before the wind chrysanthemum habitat, hands clasped behind his back in dignified fashion, and Green Hands, squatting nearby and gazing off into the distance, her head wrapped in a towel that resembled a cowl. Weathered by sun and wind, their skin retained the sleek texture of a starchy flash-steamed potato in spite of a scattering of chapped flesh. They were smiling and they looked happy.

"But there was something about them, how can I say . . . they looked almost *painfully* happy." So responded one of the photographer's assistants to a question about Bye and Green Hands.

From time to time the fervor of the visiting throngs brought a frightened look to Green Hands' face. For the memories of her loneliness, which she had never really attempted to understand, had stolen upon her like an afternoon nap.

"Well," Bye would say to her at such times, "as long as we have our magnetism we'll never be lonely again. It was so difficult before we managed to lock on to each other. But now we've finally found the Arctic."

Green Hands had another concern, less troubling but one she had never spoken of to anyone, and this was her hair. She couldn't have said with certainty when this worry had begun. Indeed, it hadn't even been a concern at first, because if you happen to lose a hair, a new one begins to grow the following day, or the day after. Hair is like the dust found anywhere in the world, like dandelion spores floating in the air, like the fog that settles thick upon a mountaintop but hides during the day, only to reemerge in the evening to embrace the mountain.

But Green Hands knew that her long hair, once it starting falling out—and she was losing several hairs a day—would not grow back. Spilling down her back, lush and dense as the closely bunched, mosslike grass of the vast steppes, her hair gradually thinned, and at a certain point she came to realize that this loss was not unrelated to the ongoing, seemingly endless proliferation of the wind chrysanthemums. And so the first thing she did, though the long hair that remained was still as glossy as the pebbles in a mountain stream, was to snip it all off and then wrap a towel around her shorn head—the towel resembling a nun's peaked hat that always identified Green Hands in the photos. She was able to do this because the loss of her hair meant very little in comparison with her

primary concern, which was to make these wind chrysanthemums the most beautiful chrysanthemums in the whole wide
world.

The more ears that "Arctic Flower" reached, the more noses
detected the wind chrysanthemum's scent and the more eyes
noticed its beauty, and in no time all those people wanted a
flower of their own to put on their windowsill. It became the
fashion for young people to offer a wind chrysanthemum to
their sweetheart on April 19, the day decades earlier when
young people had made an offering of a different sort. The
story was told of a young man who worked five months at a
gas station in order to buy a wind chrysanthemum. And there
spread a rumor that one of the flower's several scents could
increase a couple's ardor 250 percent, and although there was
no basis to this, the managers of the love hotels in the vicinity
of Seoul resorted to the black market in their desperation to
obtain that particular fragrance. This and other reports sad-
dened Bye and Green Hands.

The desire of so many people for the wind chrysanthemum
was insatiable. For Bye and Green Hands the important thing
was for the flowers, when they were about to bloom, to receive their crucial thirty-three days of Arctic wind, and even
then the fussy ones often went days past their appointed
blooming day without stirring. And so the habitat couldn't
expand as they might have hoped.

It then happened that flowers resembling the wind chrysanthemum began to appear at the markets, spawning numerous instances of confusion. These flowers had no scent
and lacked the fifty-five petals that distinguished the wind
chrysanthemum, and nowhere to be seen was the wind chrysanthemum's color—the light maroon of the delicate eyelids
of a child who has fallen asleep watching the setting sun on a

warm late-summer day. Inevitably, a few days later these fakes would wilt like any ordinary flower.

Meanwhile Tchangi had reached adulthood, at least in dog years, and he was constantly occupied with the stream of people who hid at the fringes of the habitat by day and came out at night to pilfer a wind chrysanthemum. Among the would-be flower thieves were those who, failing in their objective, would stomp on one of the flowerbeds in a fit of pique. What these people failed to realize was that the toughness of the wind chrysanthemum was centered in its roots. So even if they made off with a blossom and stuck it in a vase like they would any other flower, the rootless wind chrysanthemum would quickly lose its scent and wither away. And those who did take the time to pluck the flower by its uncommonly long roots would be detected without fail by the sharp ears of watchful Tchangi.

Horticultural enterprises arrived at Land's End promising Bye and Green Hands large sums of money if they would sign a contract granting exclusive rights for cultivation of the wind chrysanthemum at the Land's End habitat. Hard on their heels were businessmen offering a larger and higher-altitude expanse of habitat in return for the secret of cultivating the wind chrysanthemum.

The mountain on which Land's End was situated was not the most graceful. And yet its once desolate scenery had changed now that people were flocking there in droves, drawn by the wind chrysanthemum habitat, and it was now counted by many hiking clubs as one of the "best places to get away from it all." Because of the zeal of these hikers in their multi-colored outdoor wear who had tramped up the ridge to see Land's End, a row of eateries and souvenir shops now stood at the foot of the mountain. Wind chrysanthemum rice cakes and fried cakes, bearing the essence and pigmentation of the petals, sold as briskly as two-for-one T-shirts. Magic dragon stones inset with a plastic wind chrysanthemum petal, walking sticks with a flower-shaped handle, peculiar-looking back scratchers shaped like a hand and painted a light maroon— these sold as readily as the souvenir towels carrying the likeness of the wind chrysanthemum.

As high up as they lived in the mountains, Bye and Green Hands still found summer to be the most difficult season. As soon as they felt spring in the air above the woods of Land's End, they had to begin the difficult task of dividing up the wind chrysanthemum habitat into plots and in each one building a cold room in which the appropriate temperature for the flowers could be maintained. This labor exhausted Bye and Green Hands, for it meant constructing twelve cold rooms, each for flowers of a different color and a different strength of scent, and applying several coats of white paint to each structure. From afar the habitat took on the appearance of a village of igloos, and Bye would feel as if he were once again dreaming his Arctic dreams.

People continued to come to Land's End to see the exotic-looking habitat or to obtain a wind chrysanthemum. Some were so persistent in trying to use the cold rooms to escape the incessant heat that Bye had to set up a chair in the shade of the primergent tree they had planted in the yard and keep constant watch with Tchangi, who was panting like a victim of low-altitude sickness. This was also the season when the wind chrysanthemums suffered from fever, and Green Hands spent most of her time nursing them in the cold rooms.

Just how far the wind chrysanthemum craze had spread was brought home to Bye and Green Hands one viciously hot summer day. On that day the hot winds, called *masak* because they would concentrate in one place like a folded fan, had encamped right at Land's End. Two people, a man and a woman, arrived from very far away, to be greeted by the heat shimmers and the small, unseen *masak* whirlwinds.

With interpretation by Ko, who had temporarily escaped his sultry dugout, Bye and Green Hands had an extended conversation with the two visitors from abroad. Bye, thinking that he might have met for the first time in his life honest-to-God natives of the Arctic, was so excited that he proceeded to spread out the precious map he had treasured all this time. But on this map it was the Netherlands that was indicated by the man, and by the woman, whose middle finger was uncommonly long, Italy. This man and woman, having a similar destination, had taken the same trains and buses, they explained, before making the steep, hours-long climb to Land's End. They appeared to be a most unlikely pair: when one spoke, the other would either contradict or interrupt.

The man from the Netherlands repeatedly emphasized that he was a descendant of Hendrick Hamel, the first Westerner to have set foot in old Korea, who had authored a book on his experiences. Whereupon the woman from Italy proudly announced that one of her ancestors was Marco Polo, who, though prevented by unfortunate circumstances from visiting Korea, had been the first Westerner in neighboring China. Objectively speaking, she added, sweeping her fingers through her lush black hair, her forebear's *Travels* was not only better than Hamel's *Journal*, it had been written four centuries earlier. Interminable was this war of words, which made the uncommonly strong *masak* winds of that day blow even more violently. Finally, to forestall further argument, Green Hands felt compelled to hurry out and fetch a wind chrysanthemum, the variety whose strong, primeval fragrance had a mild soporific effect.

With Green Hands' intervention, Mr. Hamel and Ms. Polo regained an even keel and finally disclosed the objective of their journey to Land's End. They were both involved in a competition to procure an essence for a perfume, and had come from afar to see the wind chrysanthemum habitat, intent on using the fragrance of this flower they had until now only heard rumors of to make a perfume without precedent among the noses of the world.

Bye and Green Hands showed the couple to one of the cold rooms, and the man and woman reacted by embracing each other and producing an emotional outcry that they themselves didn't understand; it was as if they each had been flying around, all alone, in the wide blue yonder and after an absence of years had just met a longed-for friend. This was the cold room that housed the chrysanthemums that produced the scent Bye and Green Hands liked best—the Arctic scent. The couple's outburst of sentiment, though so perfectly harmonious, did not last very long.

In this first cold room, Hamel took a sniff and declared, "Smells like P-J-zero-seven-nine-six-five."

"I beg your pardon!" Polo retorted. "It's in the same family as N-H-eight-two-four-seven, popularly known as Isius—it's perfectly obvious."

"No no no—it's one our company's already developed, top secret, we haven't marketed it yet. What do you know, anyway?"

With a long, slender finger the woman tapped her upthrust nose: "This nose of mine knows anything, anywhere—and that, my dear, includes your inner thoughts."

Even as they wrangled, they wanted to visit all twelve of the cold rooms. But once they reached the second room, they no longer attempted to put each other down while classifying the scents.

"Lily-of-Saint Gabriel so pale in comparison! Rose-of-Saint Philomène so bland in contrast!"

"Garden of Pleasure! Garden of Ecstasy!"

"River of Eden! And Omphalos—Omphalos!"

Uttering these and other exclamations incomprehensible to Bye and Green Hands, the man and woman visited all the cold rooms. The couple then lapsed into silence, sat down, and stared dreamily into each other's faces. Finally, hand in hand, they left Land's End, never again to be seen there.

As you might expect, botanists were the most frequent visitors, and they came in several varieties. Some came in groups, but the majority arrived alone, posing outlandish questions to Green Hands, chewing on a wind chrysanthemum petal, or sprinkling the flowers with some sort of solution. There were those who arrived with microscopes, who would crush a petal or stamen and then examine it. No sooner did one of them leave than another would arrive, and without exception they would call out DNA-this and gene-that, cocking their heads inquisitively, and from where they sat on the edge of Bye and Green Hands' veranda they would peer suspiciously inside, as if looking for something. There were those who placed a sample of dust from the veranda in a plastic bag before leaving, and those who would deposit a handful of Land's End dirt in a bottle before proceeding straight to the well behind the habitat for a taste of the water. And those who jotted down in their notebooks the serial number, almost illegible, of the Arctic wind propeller Bye had assembled from the old-fashioned contrivances inherited from his uncle. Bye and Green Hands wouldn't have been surprised if these people had wanted one of her hairs, or a fingernail, or even a bit of her flesh. The visitors appeared all the more angry because they were doing serious research and the Land's End villagers were not helping them.

After a particularly busy weekend with a constant stream of visitors, the wind chrysanthemums suffered a breakdown.

Their ordeal was manifested in a decrease in the number of their petals, and a resulting imbalance in their aesthetic appeal and the loss of the wool from their stems. Bye and Green Hands bandaged the stalks, but some of the flowers slowly withered away nonetheless. So although the wind chrysanthemum craze had intensified, the population of wind chrysanthemums had shrunk, which, it seemed to Bye and Green Hands, would only serve to heighten the craze and draw even more people.

Bye and Green Hands were caught in a dilemma. They couldn't keep out visitors and yet they couldn't allow all the various specialists, with their overweening interest, to become a strain on the wind chrysanthemums. Fortunately Ko was there, and the Land's End villagers as well. The people of Land's End, who had looked after the wind chrysanthemum habitat almost from the start, responded to the craze by keeping out the visitors in spite of their strong protests, especially on the busy weekends, when they took turns putting aside their own work and keeping an eye on the habitat. By then it appeared that the craze had reached its peak. But there were quite a few visitors who in the face of the villagers' collective defenses stubbornly insisted on obtaining a few wind chrysanthemums before they would leave, even though the buds had not yet filled out and the leaves were still transparent.

Ko for his part had recovered from his low-altitude illness and, unbowed by the commercial failure of his Byegreen pill, he now made up his mind to devote the remainder of his life to a written account of everything related to the cultivation of Bye and Green Hands' wind chrysanthemums. Once again he withdrew to a solitary lifestyle. This decision explains why he produced so much flower writing about the wind chrysanthemum. His passion was such that he could spend a whole week on a single piece. If you lived near the habitat you would have learned that for this task he used a notebook he had produced using a secret method only he knew, and a special ink that gave off a delicate fragrance.

Because Ko kept this project a secret, there was no one in the vicinity of the habitat, except for Bye and Green Hands, who had actually seen his notebook. Ko would read aloud to others from those of his flower writings that had subsequently caught his fancy, but unfortunately only one example survives—the only evidence for future generations that the wind chrysanthemum actually existed.

Oblivious to the fact that the fresh *map'a* breezes and the hot *masak* winds had overstayed their welcome, Bye and Green Hands were totally absorbed in creating the most amazing of the fragrances they had produced thus far. They gathered eighteen ingredients—the eggs of migratory ducks, firefly wings, syringa pistils, long john callus petals, the transparent molt of alpine cicadas, and more—added them to a pool of dew, and let the mixture sit for several days. But in their effort to find the most appropriate time to water the wind chrysanthemums with this precious liquid, they several times ended up wasting it. They were constantly on the move, ranging far and wide, always searching for a better recipe.

The harsh *masak* of summer, the autumn *maya*, and the stormy early winter *mach'a*, which plucked what remained of Green Hands' hair—each of these winds scoured Land's End in turn before moving on, and one midwinter day when the whirling-dervish *mahu* was blowing, Bye and Green Hands finally engendered a wind chrysanthemum whose fragrance spread farther than all the others and was most redolent of the distant reaches of the Arctic. The scent of this newborn chrysanthemum—scent number thirteen—they called Oo-Ah.

6. *The Fate of the Wind Chrysanthemum*

"All right, everyone, can we get started? Let's save the chit-chat for later. . . . Would you kindly brief us on the agenda?"

"Yes indeed. As you can see from the report I just distributed, we—meaning the Department of Arboriculture and Horticulture—have decided on five agenda items. We have about forty minutes to discuss these, so please keep your remarks short."

"Why only forty minutes?"

"Yeah, is forty some kind of magic figure?"

"Hey, what's *this* one here?"

"That's the flower we've been talking about."

"So *that's* the one."

"Did all of you read up on it? It's one of the new and improved imports that we talked about last time, right?"

"As you can see, probably not. Now who would like to speak first? Shall we hear from the gentleman from the Pharmaceutical Association?"

"Why the Pharmaceutical Association?"

"As you know, *somebody* has to go first."

"All right, I'll try to make it short. Three of the major pharmaceutical companies are applying for a patent on wind chrysanthemum by-products. One of them is using sap from the stems to develop a treatment for respiratory conditions such as asthma, and it's supposed to be good for the alimentary system too. The second company is trying to extract a concentrate from the petals and stamens that they say can prevent dementia. And my understanding is that the third one is already marketing a urinary tract medication using the roots—the wind chrysanthemum has unusually long roots, by the way. It appears that the urinary tract medication is being marketed illegally, since it hasn't been approved yet. Our job is to consider these three medications, keeping in mind the health of our citizens, and to grant a patent for one of them. My thinking is that the urinary tract is more important than the alimentary tract, dementia is a more serious problem than urinary tract blockages, the alimentary tract is more important than dementia—"

"Will you please keep your remarks short?"

"Okay, okay, in short, the three companies that are applying for a patent are interested in three of the flower's thirteen scents—namely, number two, number seven, and number eleven. Number two is for the alimentary canal, number seven for the urinary tract, and so on . . . okay?"

"So what's the problem?"

"What's wrong with giving patents for all three?"

"What's wrong? There's only a limited number of plants—you know that."

"So why don't we grow 'em on a large scale? There must be a way to do that. Where there's a will there's a way."

"My apologies for breaking in, but I'd like to say something."

"Hang on, I'll cut to the chase. As far as the pharmaceuticals are concerned, it's inefficient having so many varieties in such a small habitat. We have to think in terms of economies of scale, for crying out loud. Shouldn't we be deciding which variety is best for our citizens' health? Once we do that we can limit cultivation to that one variety and issue the patent to the company that's developing it."

"My thoughts exactly. I suggest we discuss this agenda item first."

"As long as we keep it short and to the point."

"All right. To my mind, urinary tract ailments are the number one priority. When you gotta go, you gotta go."

"I thought somebody already developed a medication for that."

"No! You mean somebody already got a patent?"

"Excuse me, but since this is our bailiwick, so to speak, I can answer that. The medication you just mentioned is a folk remedy that someone with a very rare disease pulled out of his butt. Forget about it. This disease has a weird name—low-altitude sickness—and only one out of God knows how many millions of people has it. Far as I can tell, in the last fifty years only two cases have been reported."

"A perfect segue to what I have to say. You need to know that the number of people moving into this county is on the rise—there are all kinds of reasons, and this someone you mention is only one example—and it's creating administrative problems. I thought that since we've already hashed out the issue of applying to the Department of Arboriculture and Horticulture for funding to help these newcomers settle in, I might as well work up some figures, and I'd appreciate it if you had a look at them. That's the reason I'm here today."

"This discussion is going all over the place. Could you please be brief?"

"May I continue?"

"I should remind everyone that in the last few years a great many concerns have been lodged with us—'us' meaning the Pharmaceutical Association. There have been reports of rampant violations of government disclosure guidelines for the cultivation of plants and trees. In our horticulture laws we've always held fast to the principle of transparency regarding cultivation and technology. And I want to tell you that this wind chrysanthemum represents the most serious attack ever on the integrity of those laws—it's at the center of 80 percent of the concerns lodged with the association!"

"Before we do anything else, will you please hear me out? As all of you know, for the past year domestic cosmetics companies, in partnership with foreign counterparts, have been coming to us saying they want to extract the essence of the wind chrysanthemum and make a new fragrance out of it. They've already worked up a sales plan, complete with names for the products. According to the documents before me, names like Blue Wind, Philomène, Pôle Nord, and Omphalos have been proposed. These companies are interested in varieties four, nine, and eleven. There seems to be some overlap between this issue and the issues raised by the Pharmaceutical Association. You see, for marketing purposes the companies are emphasizing that they need to narrow down all these varieties to just one—that way there's only one perfume to produce. Between the varieties mentioned by the Pharmaceutical Association just now and the varieties that the cosmetics companies are focusing on, there's only one in common, and that's number eleven."

"The one that's good for dementia."

"Right, that's what it says in the report here."

"The thing is, none of these companies is going to back off. In the last year or so they've sunk a tremendous amount of money into R-and-D."

"It's not just the companies that aren't backing off. Isn't that why we're having this meeting?"

"How about this—can we all agree that urinary disorders are less important than dementia?"

"First, why don't we gather all these threads of conversation together, and then we'll have a solution—namely, we agree to narrow things down and focus on number eleven?"

"And if I agree, am I guaranteed funding?"

"Hey, we'll all have to deal with senility some day, so I say we go with that one."

"And then we bring in the horticulture disclosure law and apply it to number eleven and that opens the door for us to grow it big time."

"Then what about funding? The area we're talking about is under our jurisdiction, and we have to expect that more people are going to move in."

"For God's sake, will you make up your mind—is it funding you want, or fewer people moving in?"

"Actually, that's not our priority. Actually—and this is off the record—the thing is, there are several applications pending from investment companies that want to build greenbelt resorts where those plants grow . . . and it goes without saying that if these applications are granted, we'll have ourselves a swell development opportunity for our county, no doubt about it. In terms of climate and other logistics, the area is perfect for summer villas and for a ski area in the winter. To be honest, for some time now the big boys in the county administration have been thinking what an absolute waste it is for those stupid weeds to be taking up so much land."

"But isn't it the case that most of the people who moved in never obtained the necessary permit?"

"Most of them, yes. But some of them lived there before and were just moving back to where they used to live."

"I say we stop fussing about the new arrivals, bulldoze the whole goddamn area, and make it into a leisure community."

"I heard number eleven is a real noseful—what's up with that?"

"Who gives a rat's ass?"

"So you like to ski, big fella?"

"Before we finish we need to take up some old business from last time. . . . Starting with—how about I simply read the invitation we—'we' meaning the Horticulture Society—received from the International Association of Horticultural Exhibitions?'"

"Just the relevant parts, please."

"All right. 'We the International Association of Horticultural Exhibitions have a special interest in your esteemed nation's rare flower, the so-called wind chrysanthemum (scientific name undecided).' I'll skip the next part—it's too long."

"What—they haven't decided on the scientific name yet?"

"Okay, here it is. 'At our Exposition of Rare Flowers of the World, scheduled for the latter half of the current year, we wish to display seven varieties of rare flowers from your esteemed nation. In doing so we are confident of a hopeful exchange between our two nations. Particulars of this exposition will be sent in due course; upon receipt, kindly—' "

"Didn't you read that letter at the last meeting?"

"Did I? Well, the problem, according to the Department of Arboriculture and Horticulture, is that the flowers proposed by the various organizations are too different from one another. First of all, the National Garden Association limited its selections to those plants that they think best reflect our traditional culture and spirit—namely three varieties of rose-of-sharon, two varieties of pines, and two of bamboo. The Southern Horticultural Association and the Western Horticultural Association proposed flowers from their own regions, primarily orchids, and other groups made other selections, so we've got some pretty hot differences of opinion."

"This is a waste of time—didn't we take care of this stuff at the last meeting? How can we possibly have a *representative* selection of our country's plants without the rose-of-sharon?"

"But the rose-of-sharon isn't exactly a *rare* plant. This is the first time we've been invited to this exposition, and we have to abide by the conditions of the invitation."

"Well, the longer a word is, the fancier, right? So, 'representative' or 'rare,' what'll it be? Why don't we go with the longer word?"

"None of these little associations is backing off from their suggestion. I'll give an example. The domestic branch of the International Horticulture Lovers Society has sent us a list of specially developed flowers, such as our select roses, *and* the hybrid flowers that were genetically engineered by grafting the trifoliate orange with the camellia, *and* our very own wild rose—and they're demanding a representative selection of these flowers. The more difficult matter, and the thing that first caught my eye in this invitation, is, quote, 'We have a special interest in your esteemed nation's wind chrysanthemum,' et cetera, et cetera. But none of our organizations has said a single word about the wind chrysanthemum—why do you suppose that is?"

"You're beginning to sound like a shrinking violet. Listen, why don't we add the Siberian chrysanthemum? It's a very rare variety, a mutation. That'll satisfy everybody."

"How about scent number eleven?"

"Yeah, let's hear it for the senility cure!"

"Hey, everybody—what's so *representative* about the wind chrysanthemum? I'll bet it came down from North Korea and the wind carried it to that Land's End place."

"Hey, yourself. . . . Did you hear that? His accent always comes out when he gets his dander up."

"All right, as all of you can see, our forty minutes are up. Let's agree on our conclusions and call this meeting to a close."

"Which conclusions?"

"Where have you been? The conclusions we've just been talking about."

"Bye, why do people keep leaving Land's End?"

"I think they're looking for work at that theme park that's going up on the back side of the mountain."

"Bye, what do you suppose Tchangi ate that caused him to die so suddenly?"

"I think someone poisoned his food. But he's gone to a better place for sure. He had a hard life, ever since he was a puppy—remember how carsick he got when we drove up here?"

"Bye, what are we going to do about that notice from the government telling us to focus on the wind chrysanthemum with the Deep Blue scent? We can't just stop growing the other varieties, can we?"

"Nope."

"I don't want to give up any of our wind chrysanthemums. What are we supposed to do?"

"We'll come up with something tomorrow."

"If the Deep Blue chrysanthemum is the only one that's left, Mr. Ko will get sick again. If he makes his low-altitude sickness medication from that one it won't be very effective, will it?"

"Nope. But the good news is, Mr. Ko won't have to be lonesome anymore."

"That's right. He's so lucky he found someone else with low-altitude sickness. Imagine getting old and being the only one in the world with such a sickness."

"But how do you figure someone that young coming down with it?"

"People with low-altitude sickness, you can lose yourself in their eyes, right?"

"Yup."

"Why do you suppose?"

"Good question."

7. The Name-That-Species War

For more than a year now K had been analyzing the wind chrysanthemum; it had become something of a crusade with him, but when he tried to come up with conclusions he hit a wall. Here was a variety of chrysanthemum never before known! So many hours he had spent attempting to discover what about its tissue structure seemed to make it *sui generis*. It had most of the characteristics of another high-altitude species, *Chrysanthemum montuossum*, while in outward appearance it resembled *Erigeron alpicola* and *Chrysanthemum lubellum*, but in spite of these findings he had yet to unlock the secret of its mutation factor. Unless K could offer findings that revealed it, the historic task of assigning a scientific name to this rare *Gramineae* plant that went by the name wind chrysanthemum would remain unfinished.

Accompanied by his research assistants, he had made several visits to the flower's habitat. To investigate the natural conditions of the area—the amount of sunlight, rainfall, and humidity—he had staked out his research team in a dugout on the other side of the ridge, but there had been no noticeable progress in uncovering the secret. He had spoken a couple of times with the young farming couple who cultivated the wind chrysanthemums, but not only did their halting explanations fail to convince K, he had the distinct impression that part of what they told him was a fabrication—it was enough to make him want to spur the authorities to put some bite into enforcement of the horticulture disclosure laws.

And there lingered a bad taste from K's encounter with an amateur researcher who had been hanging around the habitat, the one who was writing *Everything You Wanted to Know About the Wind Chrysanthemum*. This man said he had been living at the habitat from the very beginning, that he was chronicling the history of the plant's cultivation, but far from being gracious enough to join in the grandiose project that K had initiated, he was interfering in K's work every step of the way—to the point where K felt no further need to visit the habitat.

How difficult it had become with the passing of time to discover rare plants! Each edition of the *Index Kewensis*, published by the royal botanical gardens in England, was slimmer, and the interval between one issue and the next was longer and longer. *Index Kewensis*, the compendium of botanical names issued by Kew Gardens! The very title had a kind of mythical ring to it that still made his heart jump the way it had in his thirties. You could bet your bottom *wŏn* that K's research would eventually see the light of day, and that the abstract of that research would appear in that index.

For decades K's work had taken him throughout the land as well as abroad, and he had first heard of the wind chrysanthemum, long before it became popular, from the owner of a countryside nursery whom he had met while on a lecture tour. The instant his nose detected the strong scent coming from a six-inch-tall flower, he realized it was a rare phanerogamous plant that he himself, a specialist in this field, had never seen before. Barely managing to contain his excitement, he asked the nursery owner the name of the flower and where he had acquired it.

"I got it from some people up in the mountains. They call it the wind chrysanthemum. Buy three of 'em and I'll give you a discount."

K bought three of the potted plants, then canceled the remainder of his lecture tour and went straight home.

It didn't take long for K to realize that his wind chrysanthemums had the unique effect of evoking a nostalgia that had long been hidden deep inside him. The innocent smile of his wife early in their marriage, his wife whom he had lost ten years before, came back to life; a stroll on a spring day when they were newlyweds came vividly to mind; and before he knew it K found himself weeping as he plucked the white hairs from his head.

Early in his career he'd gained fame for his research on rare plants. He'd served three consecutive terms as director of one of the most important botanical gardens in the land, and industry had capitalized on his research, so that he had become affluent early. To such a person, the reaction he was experiencing now was incomprehensible. Sad memories from his childhood, memories he had forgotten, would come back in living color and infinite beauty, and many were the days he sat in the spacious garden of his home letting them sink in. Something about those small weedlike plants he had recently added made the rest of the garden, with its preponderance of rare orchids, pale in comparison.

The feeling that this flower was fated to define his last years became an obsession for him.

"Yes, this is my final task, and the results will outlive me."

Before long he would meet his ancestors and his wife in that other world, and by then he would have published the results of his research on this flower. His ambition to incorporate his own name—the name bestowed on him by his ancestors—in the scientific name designated for this plant began to overshadow the memories of youthful failure, igniting in him a passion, the last he would ever experience, that kept him awake at night.

The failure in question came early in his career, when he was presented with an opportunity to incorporate his name in the scientific name of the recently discovered alpine sawtooth yarrow. But scarcely two months before he was to publish his research on this plant, a Japanese botanist published an article titled "The Necessity of Naming the Alpine Sawtooth Yarrow in Accordance with DNA Research." Never had he been able to forget the bitter experience of seeing his years of hard work go up in smoke. One such humiliation in his lifetime was enough.

Chrysanthemum montuossum KGB! The initials of his very own name, part of the scientific name he would bestow on the wind chrysanthemum. Though he had not been the one to discover this rare plant, he never doubted for an instant that he was the first to realize its true value. It had occurred to him to name it *Chrysanthemum venti*, keeping in mind the name by which it was popularly known—wind chrysanthemum— as well as the fact that it thrived in the wind. But that name reminded him all too clearly of the foolish young couple who insisted they had created the flower, and it was the first option he eliminated. To that young couple scientific names were as insignificant as the spores of the hillside dog dandelions sailing through the air. He, on the other hand, was firmly convinced that a scientific name should be associated with an influential scholar. And so, leaving several of his questions unanswered for the time being, he hurried to publish the results of his research in the domestic journal *Alpine Flora Abstract*, volume 45, number 2.

L's interest in the wind chrysanthemum developed later, after he got wind of these recent developments with K. By then, word of the wind chrysanthemum had spread sufficiently that L was able to take a shortcut in his own research. To L, K was a sort of growth inside him, something of which he was only subliminally aware, but that he couldn't avoid running up against in any sphere of activity in their field. There were two qualities in particular about K that L could not abide: he took himself too seriously and he was vaingloriously stubborn— the latter especially prominent in any formal setting. Both L and K had the same mentor, with L being junior to K, and at one time in their lives they had made such a good team on several projects that they looked for all the world like a honeymooning couple. But from the time that L questioned K's classification of a mutant variety of the bracken fern *Asplenium incisum*, reported those who were close to them, their relations soured.

L was busy with an agenda of his own, one he considered more important than simply pushing through a classification of the bracken fern in opposition to K's. To L it was dangerous for naïve people like K to be caught up in the strange illusion that they could stake their reputation on designating a scientific name for the wind chrysanthemum. In his youth he had dreamed of following his father and his cousin into a military career, and even though, regrettably, a broken arm sustained in a soccer match compelled him to abandon that plan, his outlook on life had already broadened and he had begun to dream of really big things. And so his interest in the wind chrysanthemum was motivated by concerns that were very different from those of K.

In his capacity as advisor to the Association for the Industrial Application of Horticultural Research, the Cooperative for the Globalization of National Phanerogamous Plants, and the Committee for Transparency in Horticulture, L had frequently been apprised, albeit indirectly, of the numerous disputes arising over the naming of the flower popularly known as the wind chrysanthemum. Then too, several organizations, which had a sufficient sense of L's long-standing love of country, his drive, and his volunteer spirit, came forward with funding for him to research the wind chrysanthemum, along with a demand for results within a short period. And so L formed a group to research the plant's distinctive characteristics and the conditions of its growth, with the goal of publishing his findings before K did his. For L the research itself was less important than the expeditious delivery of results.

And so it was that L learned of the existence of crucial research materials from an amateur researcher he had met at the wind chrysanthemum habitat. L was immediately suspicious of this person. The man claimed he suffered from low-altitude sickness, had sought out the couple who were cultivating the wind chrysanthemum, had fallen in love with this flower, and was now writing a book titled *Everything You Wanted to Know About the Wind Chrysanthemum*. L suspected that the man's true motives lay elsewhere. In any event, because this man was uniquely situated to observe the wind chrysanthemum firsthand and was recording everything about it, from the origin of its scent to the key to cultivating the distinctive coloration of its petals, L considered him indispensable.

And so L adopted a two-pronged approach: dispatching his research group to the habitat, he made a point of instructing them to extract the maximum amount of information from this man, while he himself was quick to offer what he hoped would be enticing proposals. He promised, for example, to publicize the man's remedy for low-altitude sickness, and he repeatedly had others write persuasive letters to the man containing such proposals as full funding for the publication of his book. This way he could cover himself if it proved difficult to come up with satisfactory results for the funders by the stipulated deadline; more to the point, it would be possible for him to appropriate that man's knowledge about the wind chrysanthemum.

In truth, L was not that interested in such matters as establishing scientific names. Still, he could not simply stand by until the day arrived when *Chrysanthemum montuossum KGB* became official. Why in God's name did K's initials have to be KGB? Didn't he realize that future generations would assume that the plant came from the dark, damp regions of the former Soviet Union? If you were going to designate the scientific name for that plant, it would have to be something on the order of *Chrysanthemum coreanum*. Sure, if he pushed his research a bit more, he could incorporate his own name, but he preferred instead to use the name of his country. Deferring to the nation was in keeping with a long-standing family precept, and indeed L rather delighted in such self-sacrifice.

On the assumption that his choice for a scientific name would be accepted, and to publicize the flower more widely, he had it recommended for the National Rare Flower Show and the Special Exhibition of Alpine Plants, both of which he had been invited to adjudicate. Observing the formality of making public his group's research, he sent a letter to the editorial board of the *Proceedings of the 78th International Convention for Plant Geography* informing them of his intention to publish his findings—even though the research itself was not yet concluded.

Chrysanthemum montuossum KGB! Chrysanthemum coreanum! M muttered to himself scornfully as he shaved for the first time in three days—his beard felt like a rug. He screwed up his face as he wielded the razor, unintentionally making a wry smile. M liked to shave whenever he had a weighty decision on his hands. Freshly smooth, he phoned the lab for a progress report, hoping for at least a few tidbits of information from the previous day's work. But there was nothing to report—nor had there been the day before. Granted, he wasn't expecting miracles from his outmoded laboratory and its outmoded apparatus, but he couldn't understand why in his lab alone all indications were that this supposedly exceptionally rare flower, which had everyone in such a tizzy, was a perfectly commonplace variety of chrysanthemum.

M then called several businesses that had expressed a commercial interest in the wind chrysanthemum. The crucial matter here was patents, and he learned from these calls that none of the companies had yet obtained one. The window of opportunity was still open, and it was time for him to take a decisive step.

M was one of the lesser known and less ambitious botanists. L, from the same hometown as he; K, who had always regarded him as a conniving fake; and a few others as well, N, O, and P—these specialists had jumped on the research bandwagon for this phanerogamous plant at the height of its popularity, but not until recently had this fact motivated M himself. L's face came to mind, the face of the man who always held sway in grandiose fashion at the annual dinner party for the hometown luminaries. To be sure, it was an irritant, but M's decision to plunge into the name-that-species war was not because of this unpleasant reminder of L, nor was it a question of popularity—M was not one to be caught up in fads. Rather, by naming the flower M could proudly lay claim to all manner of patents. Which in turn would mean the renovation of his outmoded lab! And updated equipment! These were M's hoped-for spoils of war.

M was a perceptive sort. From his vantage point, L was a puffed-up man who fancied himself the hero and because of this could never keep a secret, and this was his weak point. As for K, he was overly proud and this was a huge flaw, but M's intuition told him that as long as he avoided injuring that pride he could persuade the man, unlike L, to help him.

M was sensitive about his appearance, and on this day, as all others, he inspected himself in the mirror. He was dressed in blue jeans and a green Polo shirt, not wanting to make the people at the wind chrysanthemum habitat feel inferior. One last time he mentally reviewed his plan. He wondered if it was wishful thinking, the impression he'd gotten from the people who lived at Land's End and who cultivated the wind chrysanthemum, that they favored him alone—for they were rumored to be quite fussy. At the same time, he trusted in his sociable appearance and his capabilities.

He had a business deal he would propose to the couple who cultivated the wind chrysanthemum: they would give him essential information for his research, and then when he published his findings he would use whatever scientific name for the plant they wished. Of course he'd also have to mention the business angle, so he had jotted down in his appointment book enough particulars for him to give a simplified explanation of such complicated matters as the division of royalties from the patents. They couldn't have known this, but he already had a name in mind for the flower, a name so beautiful that the boring names proposed by K and L—well, what else could you expect from *them?*—simply could not compare. *Chrysanthemum ventiphaerum*—chrysanthemum suffused with wind! How poetic, how alpine! If the couple who cultivated the wind chrysanthemum were at all sensitive to the beauty of the plant world, then their first reaction to the name would be a stirring of the blood. And if they preferred "Arctic Flower," no problem, he had a scientific name for that one too—*Chrysanthemum arcticum*. Didn't they call her Green Hands, the young woman who was the repository of all the secrets of the plant's cultivation? He could take that name and suggest

Chrysanthemum azureum. With that thought, M started up his car.

"Bye, is it a long way to the Arctic?"

"Yup."

"Can we get there on a full tank of gas?"

"We might have to ditch the truck midway and make ourselves a raft."

"We'll have to learn how to steer it."

"Yup."

"Won't we lose our magnetic power if we're traveling over water?"

"If we leave on a stormy day we'll be all right. There's magnetic power in lightning."

"Bye, can flowers bloom in the Arctic?"

"Sure, I've seen 'em in photos."

"Bye, when we get to the Arctic I'm going to call our flower the Arctic flower instead of the wind chrysanthemum."

"Fine, Green Hands, let's do that."

8. The Demise of the Wind Chrysanthemum

If not for a most unexpected development, the skirmish over the scientific name for the wind chrysanthemum would have been even longer and more complicated. At a time when K, L, and M were advancing their respective plans, L was the first to get wind of this development, and for him it was catastrophic—a rejection letter from the editorial board of the *Proceedings of the 78th International Convention for Plant Geography*:

It is with the utmost regret that we inform you that an article on the flower on which you proposed to publish, tentatively designated *Chrysanthemum coreanum*, has been published in the *New Journal of Botany* (volume 37, number 2). . . .

There were no further particulars. Finishing this short letter, L immediately assumed the author of the article was K, and a passionate hatred of the man swept over him. Not long afterward he found in his mailbox a copy of the journal; there was no return address. He ripped open the envelope and quickly scanned the contents page. There it was, "A Physiological Approach to *Chrysanthemum multiodoratum Byegreen*," but the author was a man named A, unknown to him, and no affiliation or biographical details were given. L proceeded straight to the conclusion of the article, like an equestrian whipping his steed over the final jump.

The peculiar scientific name proposed by A meant "Byegreen chrysanthemum having various scents"—hence *Chrysanthemum multiodoratum Byegreen*. Too impatient to read enough of the article to learn the reason for this name, L hurled the journal to the floor. Then he picked it up and, with muscles toned through exercise, heaved it into his wastebasket.

The next to know was K, a regular subscriber to the *New Journal of Botany*, and he too was astonished. His face turned the sickly color of paper under yellow light; his nose prickled at the strong scent of his own wind chrysanthemum, its petals gently moving in the spring breeze where it sat on his coffee table; the strange emotion he felt on this particular day brought him to tears; and this improbable combination made him sick to his stomach. In spite of the hot tears blurring his vision, he read the article at what felt to him like the speed of light. Why was he crying? It was true that he felt like a sad sack whenever he breathed in the fragrance of the wind chrysanthemum, but it was also true that at this moment he was hopping mad. Who the hell was this A guy, and how had someone in the same country published a paper that started with an argument half similar to the argument in a research paper he himself had already published? In this country and in this field there couldn't be a specialist he didn't know about. Conveniently ignoring the fact that A's paper had solved the points he had racked his brains over, he decided that A had plagiarized. Taking a tranquilizer, as he usually did when delicate matters erupted, he gazed out, somber-faced, at his garden. Another humiliation? Never! So now—how could he negate the other man's accomplishment? That was the question.

M's case was different. He was a person who cherished his precious optimism, who wasn't hurt by insignificant matters, but thanks more than anything else to his prudent nature, he didn't live in constant fear that one day, out of the blue, one of the assistants at his lab would thrust a paper like this one under his nose. And he wasn't lacking in backbone, wouldn't easily give up something he had started. So he set out at once to take protective measures for his problem solving, his data collecting, and the delicate matters on which the future of the dozen employees of his lab depended.

As he did every morning, he began this distasteful day with a round of phone calls. His relations with others always had to be tended to—it was like polishing a piece of fine celadon—so he never skipped these calls unless he was very ill. He mobilized his usual acquaintances and asked them to find out what they could about this man A. He was of a mind to call K and L right then and there, but his intuition told him to hold back for the time being. He threw himself into shaving as he went over in his head the day's work.

He was struck by a thought. Razor in hand, he dashed to his study, where he took a thick file from his desk drawer and

carefully inspected the materials relating to the wind chrysanthemum. He was more or less finished when the phone calls
began to come in from the friends he had asked to make inquiries about A. He learned through these calls that K and L
were also making inquiries, and although he could imagine,
as if he were seeing it right before his eyes, the rage that was
sweeping over them, this elicited no twisted satisfaction in
him.

Most of what he learned from his informants concerned
the background of this young, unknown scholar named A.
Few of them had anything to offer about how A was proceeding with his research and how he had arrived at his results.
But there was one who could give a detailed report on A's
background. According to this source, the paper in question
had not been sent in to the *New Journal of Botany* by A himself. A had briefly studied abroad, and had sent a draft of the
paper to a colleague he had gotten to know at that time, and
from there it had ended up in the journal. To M this sounded
like a childish rumor. But there were contradictions in what
his informants were telling him, enough to make his head
swim. One thing was certain: the fates of K, L, and himself
were as firmly connected to one another as barnacles to a
rock.

Unlike his usual urgency on the phone, he was composed
as he made notes on what he had learned. One common
thread revealed in this babel of information was the banal fact
that A was an average, everyday person.

At the conclusion of all the phone calls M summarized
what he had learned about A: 5'8" tall, 116 pounds in weight.
Close acquaintances had been heard to say he was a devoted
and gentle sort; an introvert, didn't like doing things in public, took pleasure in the anonymity of travel. Parents raised
pigs for a living. An exceptional case of success in circum-

stances that were far from easy. Spent two years at the University of Amsterdam on a scholarship, returned home and found a teaching job at his alma mater in C Province. One son, two daughters. Sphere of activity was narrow, didn't belong to any scholarly associations, was a member of only one organization—the National *Paduk* Lovers' Association. Two books: *A History of Botany* and *The Range of Dicotyledon Arbor Plants in C Province*. A dozen published essays, none attracting much attention. "A Physiological Approach to *Chrysanthemum multiodoratum Byegreen*," recently published in the *New Journal of Botany*, his first paper on the *Gramineae* family of plants.

K and L obtained similar information about A. K, as soon as he had regained a modicum of composure, began a letter of protest to A, a letter that spoke resolutely of the importance of rigor and transparency in research. It could not be more regrettable, he wrote, that his esteemed counterpart's essay contained more than half of an article he himself had already published, and if a public apology and redress for this ethical lapse were not forthcoming at an early date, then for the sake of future generations he would have to consider legal action. It was a long letter. K hoped it would inspire in its recipient the most impressive sentiments of any letter he had written. The last thing he did, to further deepen those sentiments in any who might read this after his death, was to touch up a few places with editorial passion. Before putting the letter in an envelope, he decided he would read it aloud from beginning to end, his tone of voice appropriate to the contents. It so happened just then that the fragrance of his wind chrysanthemum reminded him of a letter he had written decades ago but never sent, and his voice almost broke. But he went on reading.

L for his part put on a record of martial music and turned the volume all the way up. Chin resting on his palm, he gave himself up to the fierce intensity aroused in him by the music, the beauty of its regularity and its repetition. This was the reason he liked all kinds of marches. Hah! *Chrysanthemum multiodoratum Byegreen*—was that what he was calling it? How shortsighted, how aesthetically barren in contrast with *Chrysanthemum coreanum*. And he probably didn't like marching music either. L was suspicious of types who upset that which was regular, and his sense that it was his mission to punish them was doubled by the music and transformed into a thunderous drumming that pounded away in his very heart. But he couldn't put into words just what sort of regularity this guy A had upset. In an effort to articulate this point to himself he listened to the record again and again—so truly did he like repetition.

The wind chrysanthemum craze was met with a headwind that strengthened to gale force in what seemed like a split second. Nobody knew or could say what the source of that headwind was. There were several possibilities, but it was very difficult to single out any one and say, "*That's* where it blew in from." Like all winds, it was a thing of nature, a sweeping mass of self-generating energy. With the speed of a hot desert wind that covers a caravan track with dunes of sand, it blew throughout the country—with the exception of the wind chrysanthemum habitat—turning people's minds topsy-turvy in a matter of moments.

It started with numerous rumors about the very same wind chrysanthemum that, for the fortunate ones, had occupied their garden, living room, windowsill, or study, captivating the owners of those spaces with daytime reveries of endless sweetness—and those rumors made tongues wag like the fluttering of tiger moths on a summer night. The Ocean scent, which prompted profound introspection; the Cloud scent, which comforted unsettled souls; the Oo-Ah scent, which brought to the ear the music of a celestial dance— people now cited one instance after another of the dangers these fragrances posed to the human mind and body. Someone claimed that the wind chrysanthemum was a variety of poppy containing narcotic elements. An example was cited of the deviant behavior of adolescent girls who stole from their parents' wallets in order to obtain a wind chrysanthemum. The sap of the wind chrysanthemum stems, efficacious in the treatment of urinary disorders and dementia; the roots and the extract of its petals and stamens—contained in these very same substances were elements that worsened gastric cramps, nervous disorders, and constipation. Such rumors made people afraid even to set eyes on a wind chrysanthemum.

Articles appeared in magazines commenting on before-and-after photos of the couple who grew the wind chrysanthemums and warning that because of certain elements in the flowers, if you merely looked at or smelled one of them, your hair would fall out. Word got around that the Health Administration would launch an investigation into claims about the negative effects of the wind chrysanthemum, and that the findings would result in the closing down of the habitat. These had the effect of doubling the speed of this sudden headwind.

Around this time an article appeared in the science section of one of the daily newspapers together with a photo of three scientists with their hands clasped together—K, L, and M— and the caption "Long Separation, Meaningful Reunion." The article was about their recently published joint work, *A Study of the Wind Chrysanthemum*, and it praised the three authors to the skies. These men, estranged for more than a decade by the competition among them, had refused to isolate themselves in their research centers and laboratories and had instead come together in a joint research project in order to wipe out all the misunderstandings about this plant that had become an object of such widespread interest. In so doing they would offer a sound path for the future. The article quoted L as saying,

> Our joint interest in the wind chrysanthemum as an object of research and our commonality of viewpoint are inspired by the spirit of mutual cooperation we once enjoyed but had lost for some time, and so it happened that this book was published jointly. Ironically enough, this wind chrysanthemum has become a symbol of peace and reconciliation among the three of us. We shouldn't forget that M and myself are from the same hometown, and K and I were nurtured by the same mentor—you might say we're brothers in study.

Research on the physiology of the wind chrysanthemum took up the first part of the book, while the second part merely offered instances hinting indirectly at how unrealistic and unscientific were the brazen attempts to capitalize on the plant in one area or another. Even so, its publication and the modest article about it came at the perfect time, the book being perceived by readers as playing a huge role in debunking the numerous rumors and wild speculation spreading along with the headwind that blew against the wind chrysanthemum.

Amid the huge swirl of this headwind, A published an opposing view. This defense of the wind chrysanthemum drew no particular attention apart from fomenting a conspiracy theory within a group that had invested considerable funds in commercializing the flower.

It never became necessary to prohibit sales of the wind chrysanthemum and the various items developed from it that had been selling so well. Those who had bought so feverishly were now coming forward with claims for damages suffered, but because there were numerous opportunists who suffered hereditary hair loss, chronic heart disease, and other maladies unrelated to the wind chrysanthemum, the cruel aftermath of the headwind did not extend to such calamities as requiring the young couple who cultivated the plant to take legal responsibility, pay damages, or go to jail.

Even so, the residents of the county to which Land's End belonged demanded that the wind chrysanthemum habitat be closed so that they might see the region developed and its environment protected, and to this end they staged heated protests outside the county offices. The county executive was able to disperse the protestors with a promise to meet their demands at an early date. The greenbelt resort was by now a *fait accompli*.

Several months after the arrival of the headwind, the wind chrysanthemum habitat was closed down, and this rare variety of chrysanthemum ceased to be grown in Land's End and indeed the world at large. As for articles about the wind chrysanthemum, there survive today only the essay by A, which after its publication overseas was never republished domestically, and the single example of flower writing by Ko, the low-altitude sickness patient who was befriended by the young couple and lived at the habitat.

And then there was *Everything You Wanted to Know About the Wind Chrysanthemum*, but the notebook in which Ko had written it—made of a paperlike substance composed of leaves bleached and dried, written with ink utilizing the light maroon color of the petals—survived not much longer than the plant itself. The author of this peculiar notebook had intended for it to be preserved, but, absurdly, it was stolen one day. It was the destiny of those peculiar leafy pages to die a slow death, quite apart from any effect of the headwind. For the notebook ended up in the hands of senior citizens who still believed the old rumor that wind chrysanthemum leaves afforded protection against dementia, and the fate of those pages was to be rolled into cigarettes and to go up in smoke.

9. North Pole Traveling

The night was uncommonly dark at the ocean shore. An unseasonable storm had arrived. Snatches of a duet from *Tristan und Isolde* escaped through the open window of an unlit seaside villa. On the windowsill sat a man, seemingly oblivious to the driving wind and rain, gazing at the long outline of the coast, which came in and out of sight through the storm. The low-pitched, solemn voices of the two lovers carried along the shore as if to soothe the storm, which was shaking heaven and earth:

> Descend upon us, O night of love,
> Make me forget that I live.
> Take me up into your bosom,
> release me from the world!

A small truck trundled into view from the east, a single headlight burning faintly. It shuffled down to the shore and came to a stop.

Holy twilight's glorious imminence
makes imagined terrors melt away,
freeing us from the world.

Two silhouettes emerged from the truck, flickered in and
out of view within the storm, and moved off into the thicker
gloom of the ocean. Hand in hand, the silhouettes walked into
the mountainous, cresting waves—or so it appeared to the
man perched on the windowsill. He wasn't that concerned.
Young lovers and ocean storms go together, he reassured himself.

Heart to heart, mouth on mouth,
bound together in a single breath . . .
the world . . . lit by day's deception.

At the next driving gust of wind and rain, the truck's
headlight went out for good. The darkness enveloping the
oceanside was thicker now and the duet of Tristan and Isolde
louder, as if in defiance of the frenzied storm. How far would
the two voices travel along the coastline? Would the two
silhouettes emerge from the water? The man listening to the
music didn't know. Nor could he see anything.

Then am I myself the world;
floating in sublime bliss,
life of love most sacred,
never again to waken,
free of delusion, sweetly conscious desire.

A peal of thunder in the distance. A white cockscomb of
lightning cleaved the heavens and briefly illuminated the
nondescript truck before fading away. The man at the windowsill disappeared to turn over the record.

The following day, when the wind and rain had given way to sunshine, the truck was still there, and so too the day after.

Nobody arrived to claim it.

The local children used it as a play space, with its compass and tattered map and scattering of seeds, until the man who looked after the beach had it towed away.

The translators acknowledge the assistance of the Banff International Literary Translation Centre at The Banff Centre in Banff, Alberta, Canada.

Afterword

The three stories in this volume span the first decade of Ch'oe Yun's career as a creative writer. The title story, appearing first in the summer 1988 issue of *Munhak kwa sahoe* (Literature and society), was her very first published work of literature (she had previously published literary criticism). In its sophisticated and polyphonic narrative, its inspiration by one of the most horrific events in modern Korean history, and its skillful treatment of trauma, *There a Petal Silently Falls* is one of the strongest debut works in modern Korean literature. Interested, like Bakhtin, in polyphonic narratives, Ch'oe tells this story in three voices: a third-person narrative from the viewpoint of an inarticulate construction worker, the first-person narrative of a traumatized girl, and a plural first-person narrative related by a group of college students who are retracing the girl's steps in an effort to locate her. Although the novella was inspired by the Kwangju massacre of May 1980, it is not about that event as much as it is an inquiry into how such outrages can happen. A central theme in the story is the psychology of abuse and violence at the level of both the individual and the state, with the construction worker and the girl representing the victimizer and the victim, respectively. The structure of the story is cyclical, with both the girl and the student group en route to possible healing and closure.

"Whisper Yet" (Soksagim soksagim, first published in November 1993 in *Hanguk munhak* [Korean literature]), is a retrospective narrative that takes up a familiar motif in post–1945 Korean fiction—that of a divided land. In this story the division is both geographical and ideological, featuring an ironic bonding between the narrator's father—an anti-Communist refugee from North Korea living in the South—and Ajaebi, a pro-Communist native of the South who is a fugitive. The narrative frame consists of the narrator's silent dialogue with her daughter during a vacation in a countryside orchard, much like the orchard where the narrator spent her formative years in the company of Ajaebi. During this vacation, the narrator reconstructs the story of Ajaebi's life as orchard caretaker, separated from his own family by his fugitive status.

"The Thirteen-Scent Flower" (Yolse kaji irŭm ŭi kkot hyanggi, first published in the summer 1995 issue of *Munhak kwa sahoe*), is a bravura piece that displays Ch'oe's familiarity with postmodern writing and her concern with the commercialization of contemporary South Korean society. Ch'oe is a strongly intertextual writer, having authored stories with such titles as "Hanyorŭm naj ŭi kkum" (1989, A midsummer day's dream), "P'andora ŭi kabang" (1991, Pandora's box), "Woshingt'on kwangjang (1993, Washington Square), and "P'urŭn kich'a (1994, Blue train). Sharp-eyed readers of the present story will notice a reference to Albert Hitchcock, several portmanteau words, and excerpts from a Wagner opera that may help situate the unusual relationship between Bye and Green Hands. (For the excerpts from the love duet in Act 2 of Wagner's *Tristan und Isolde*, quoted in section 9 of "The Thirteen-Scent Flower," we have drawn on two sources: pages 175, 177, and 179 of the unattributed English libretto in the 267-page "booklet," edited by Peter Quantrill, for the 2005 EMI Classics CD/DVD version of the opera; and the unattributed subtitles of the 2005 Opus Arte DVD version of the opera.)

Ch'oe Yun is a writer for the new millennium, an articulate and prescient observer of a traditional agrarian society caught in the winds of the political, socioeconomic, and cultural changes so skillfully parodied in "The Thirteen-Scent Flower." She is also intensely interested in the possibilities of fiction and constantly experiments with her narratives— for example, in her ongoing project of very short quasi-autobiographical writings collectively titled *Chajŏn p'ap'yŏn* (Self-fragments). As she approaches her third decade of creative writing, we can expect her to continue to push the thematic and narrative boundaries of contemporary Korean fiction.

Suggestions for Further Reading

Ch'oe Yun. "The Gray Snowman." Trans. Bruce and Ju-Chan Fulton. In *Modern Korean Fiction: An Anthology*, ed. Bruce Fulton and Youngmin Kwon, 345–70. New York: Columbia University Press, 2005.

———. "The Last of Hanak'o." Trans. Bruce and Ju-Chan Fulton. In *Land of Exile: Contemporary Korean Fiction*, rev. and exp. ed., trans. and ed. Marshall R. Pihl and Bruce and Ju-Chan Fulton, 276–96. Armonk, N.Y.: M. E. Sharpe, 2007.

Fulton, Bruce. "Ch'oe Yun." In *The Columbia Companion to East Asian Literature*, ed. Joshua Mostow, 740–42. New York: Columbia University Press, 2003.

Fulton, Bruce and Ju-Chan. "Infinity Through Language: A Conversation with Ch'oe Yun." *Korean Culture* 17, no. 4 (Winter 1996): 5–7.

Scott-Stokes, Henry, and Lee Jae Eui, eds. *The Kwangju Uprising: Press Accounts of Korea's Tiananmen*. Armonk, N.Y.: M. E. Sharpe, 2000.

Shin, Gi-wook and Kyung Moon Hwang, eds. *Contentious Kwangju: The May 18 Uprising in Korea's Past and Present*. Lanham, Md.: Rowman & Littlefield, 2003. See in particular the section titled "Literature" (92–97) in Don Baker's essay "Victims and Heroes: Competing Visions of May 18" (87–107).